"So, how do you feel about being the mother of my children?"

Angelo asked innocently.

Coffee lodged in Allison's throat. She coughed, staring incredulously at the man sitting across from her.

He firmly patted her on the back and urged a glass of water on her.

"Are you ready to answer my question?" he asked with a grin.

"I don't think it deserves an answer," she said when she could speak again.

"Is that another way of saying you'll think about it?" *A little girl,* he decided. *They'd have a little girl first. And she'd look just like Allison.*

"I can't figure out if you're making some sort of joke or you're just plain crazy," she finally said.

"Isn't there another choice?"

"Such as?" she asked suspiciously.

"My being head over heels in love with you."

D0054634

Dear Reader,

It's that time of year again—pink hearts, red roses and sweet dreams abound as we celebrate that most amorous of holidays—St. Valentine's Day!

Silhouette Romance captures the sentimental mood of the month with six new tales of lovers who are meant for each other—and even if *they* don't realize it from the start, *you* will!

Last month, we launched our new FABULOUS FATHERS series with the first heartwarming tale of fatherhood. Now, we bring you the second title in the series, *Uncle Daddy.* Popular author Kasey Michaels has packed this story with humor and emotion as hero Gabe Logan learns to be a father—and a husband.

Also in February, Elizabeth August's *The Virgin Wife* whisks you away to Smytheshire, a fictional town where something dark and secret is going on. Once you've been there, you'll want to visit this wonderful, intriguing place again—and you can! Be sure to look for other Smytheshire books coming in the near future from Elizabeth August and Silhouette Romance.

To complete this month's offerings, we have book one of Laurie Paige's new ALL-AMERICAN SWEETHEARTS series, *Cara's Beloved,* as well as *To the Rescue* by Kristina Logan, *Headed for Trouble* by Joan Smith and Marie Ferrarella's *Babies on His Mind.*

In months to come, we'll be bringing you books by all your favorite authors—Diana Palmer, Annette Broadrick, Suzanne Carey and more! In the meantime, we at Silhouette Romance wish you a Happy Valentine's Day spent with someone special!

Anne Canadeo
Senior Editor

BABIES ON HIS MIND

Marie Ferrarella

Silhouette
R O M A N C E™
Published by Silhouette Books New York
America's Publisher of Contemporary Romance

If you purchased this book without a cover you should be aware that this book is stolen property. It was reported as "unsold and destroyed" to the publisher, and neither the author nor the publisher has received any payment for this "stripped book."

To Richard, the last of the Ferrarella men to be captured. And to Susan, welcome to the clan.

SILHOUETTE BOOKS
300 E. 42nd St., New York, N.Y. 10017

BABIES ON HIS MIND

Copyright © 1993 by Marie Rydzynski-Ferrarella

All rights reserved. Except for use in any review, the reproduction or utilization of this work in whole or in part in any form by any electronic, mechanical or other means, now known or hereafter invented, including xerography, photocopying and recording, or in any information storage or retrieval system, is forbidden without the permission of the publisher, Silhouette Books, 300 E. 42nd St., New York, N.Y. 10017

ISBN: 0-373-08920-1

First Silhouette Books printing February 1993

All the characters in this book have no existence outside the imagination of the author and have no relation whatsoever to anyone bearing the same name or names. They are not even distantly inspired by any individual known or unknown to the author, and all incidents are pure invention.

®: Trademark used under license and registered in the United States Patent and Trademark Office and in other countries.

Printed in the U.S.A.

Books by Marie Ferrarella

Silhouette Romance

The Gift #588
Five-Alarm Affair #613
Heart to Heart #632
Mother for Hire #686
Borrowed Baby #730
Her Special Angel #744
*The Undoing of
Justin Starbuck* #766
Man Trouble #815
The Taming of the Teen #839
Father Goose #869
Babies on His Mind #920

Silhouette Special Edition

It Happened One Night #597
A Girl's Best Friend #652
Blessing in Disguise #675
Someone To Talk To #703
World's Greatest Dad #767

Silhouette Books

Silhouette Christmas Stories 1992
"The Night Santa Claus Returned"

Books by Marie Ferrarella writing as Marie Nicole

Silhouette Romance

Man Undercover #373
Please Stand By #394
Mine by Write #411
Getting Physical #440

Silhouette Desire

Tried and True #112
Buyer Beware #142
Through Laughter and Tears #161
Grand Theft: Heart #182
A Woman of Integrity #197
Country Blue #224
Last Year's Hunk #274
Foxy Lady #315
Chocolate Dreams #346
No Laughing Matter #382

MARIE FERRARELLA

was born in Europe, raised in New York City and now lives in Southern California. She describes herself as the tired mother of two overenergetic children and the contented wife of one wonderful man. She is thrilled to be following her dream of writing full-time.

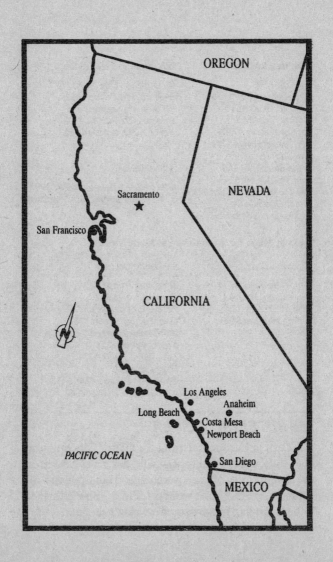

Chapter One

It was Fate that brought them together that Friday morning in Bedford, throwing them against each other suddenly in an unexpected, lightning-flash meeting that left a definite impression on Angelo Marino's mind as well as his body.

Angelo was alone, reclining on the grass, staring up at an incredibly blue sky and contemplating the very nature of his existence for the first time in thirty-six years. In the background was the sound of small children playing under the watchful eyes of their mothers at the park across the street from his garden apartment. It was the sight and the sound of the children that had triggered his thoughtful mood, although he knew it had been a long time in the making.

One moment he was alone, the next Angelo found himself part of an entangled threesome.

Fate came in the shape of a hundred-and-fifteen-pound tan Great Dane. Hers.

Up until he had large paw prints on the upper part of the torso he religiously kept in top condition, Angelo had been

trying very hard to drain his mind and body of all thought
and, particularly, all tension. It had just begun to work
when Fate ran right over him, dragging his owner in his
wake.

"Wait, stop," a woman's voice pleaded. Later that day,
when he played the words over in his head, Angelo realized
that she hadn't pleaded. She had issued a soft, firm command. One that went totally unheeded as the Great Dane
stumbled onto Angelo. *Then* the dog had stopped abruptly,
his heavy frame outlining Angelo's. Newton's laws of
physics stated that a body in motion tended to stay in motion unless acted upon by an external force. When the dog
stopped moving, the woman who was attached to his leash
continued going until she met that external force—Angelo.

With the air temporarily knocked out of him, Angelo
looked straight into the most beautiful pair of blue eyes he
had ever seen. Her face was inches away from his. Ach-
ingly close. If the breath hadn't been knocked out of him by
the dog, it would have left now in a whoosh of surprise and
genuine appreciation.

The dog, bless him, had jerked to the side, and suddenly
there was just the two of them, Adam and Eve, their bodies
touching at all the points that God had created for just this
moment, Angelo thought, a rush of desire sweeping through
him at a stunning pace.

Opportunity had never knocked to find Angelo not at
home. He threw the door open now. With his arm tighten-
ing quickly around her to keep this angel that had dropped
out of the sky from spilling onto the ground next to him, it
took every shred of control Angelo possessed not to brush
his lips lightly against hers. She smelled of berries. Strawberries. And of spring in the midst of what had been a long,
hot summer.

Removing a leaf from her hair, he grinned. "Are you
hurt?" She certainly didn't feel hurt, he thought. She felt
wonderful. He made no move to rise. Maybe he'd stay like

this until Christmas, he mused, twirling the stem of the leaf between his thumb and forefinger.

Yanking away with a surprised gasp, Allison Conrad scrambled to her feet. Her legs felt shaky. All of her did. The brief, unexpected encounter with this hard-as-rock male had completely undone her, depleting her air supply and replacing it with something totally unsettling. Dragging air into her lungs, Allison quickly brushed grass out of her hair and from her clothes. From the scent she guessed that the grass must have been mowed recently. Sliced blades of grass were peppered all over her jogging outfit.

She realized that the man on the ground was watching her intently and with a good deal of amusement in his eyes. Allison stopped dusting off her body.

As if sensing the thoughts running through Angelo's mind, the Great Dane moved back until his legs formed a parenthesis around Angelo's body.

Allison couldn't help the laugh that surfaced as she looked at Angelo's surprised expression. "I should be asking you if you're hurt."

Her laugh was soft and throaty, reinforcing the sensuous feelings that were pulsing through him. "Then ask." He'd listen to anything she'd say.

Allison leaned down. This time her face remained a safe distance from Angelo's. "Are you all right?"

Angelo glanced at the dog's square tan muzzle. If he had his druthers, he'd definitely prefer having the woman on top of him instead of this beast.

"I've been better." Angelo attempted to move the obstacle from him and the dog growled, low and obviously displeased. He quickly withdrew his hands, holding them aloft. "Lots better. Could you get him to, maybe move?"

She liked having the advantage. That one unguarded moment on top of the dark-haired stranger had made her uncomfortably aware of things she thought she had successfully kept locked away.

"Oh, I'm sorry." She rose to her feet, picking up the dog's leash. Brushing a single wayward wisp of hair from her face, she gave the leash one small tug. "Fate, heel."

As if he were no more than a docile, obedient puppy, the dog stepped lightly over Angelo and stood at his mistress's side.

The picture of woman and dog was formidable and Angelo had a suspicion that she knew it. He got to his feet quickly, brushing off the grass he had accumulated. Then he looked at the dog. "Fate?"

The man hadn't seemed that tall a moment ago. Lying on the ground, he had looked shorter. Height somehow tipped the scale in his favor. She had no idea why she felt so threatened. She was safe enough. Allison raised her chin, subconsciously trying to compensate for the difference in stature. "Someone left him on my doorstep as a puppy." She remembered how displeased her father had been. It was the only time she had ever asked him for something. Pleaded, really. He had finally relented but had never let her forget it. Allison ran her hand over the dog's head as she smiled at the animal. "I decided it was Fate that brought us together."

He caught himself wishing that she'd look at him like that. Angelo Marino, envious of a dog. He was really going to have to take stock of his life, he thought. "Funny you should mention that."

Her blue eyes darkened ever so slightly as she looked at Angelo. She looked at the hard ridges of muscle that his washed-out T-shirt accentuated rather than hid. Her fingers tightened around the leash. "What?"

He didn't think she'd appreciate being let in on his thoughts. Yet. "Just mumbling."

She could feel his long, sweeping look as it passed over her, feel it just as much as she had the contours of his body for that brief moment she had been on top of him. Remembering made her heart begin to hammer again, just the way it had when she fell on him. The run she had squeezed in this morning was supposed to invigorate her, not throw her completely out of kilter. What was the matter with her?

She was about to leave. He could tell by the way she shifted her weight to the balls of her feet. "Do you do this often?" He gestured at her jogging clothes. "Jog, I mean, not fall on top of people."

Allison thought of the desk full of papers waiting for her attention. The meeting that was only a few hours away. So many demands, so little time. "Not often enough."

She sounded wistful. Angelo looked at her clothes. She was wearing a jogging outfit. It wasn't meant to make a fashion statement the way so many of the ones he had seen were. She obviously exercised in it. The colors, if they could be called that, were so badly faded that it was hard to determine just what shade they had initially been. Her blond hair fell loosely around her face. The sweatshirt was baggy, but the waist he had momentarily touched was small. It would seem that she managed to sneak in enough time to sculpt a figure that could make a man's mouth water. And spin dreams in his head. The way dreams were spinning in his.

She couldn't explain why, but he was making her nervous. If he was dangerous, she knew that Fate would have detected it and been growling. And yet she had a feeling that this man *was* somehow dangerous and the sooner she got away, the better.

Allison looked at her watch. If she didn't get back home and grab a quick shower now, she was going to be late for the meeting.

"Well, I'd better be going." Wrapping the leash around her hand firmly, Allison turned, ready to jog out of his life as quickly as she had come into it.

Angelo's hand darted out as he grabbed her wrist. "Wait, I didn't catch your name."

Allison looked down at her wrist expectantly, but he didn't release it. Her chin rose defiantly again. "I didn't throw it."

Because the contact seemed to bother her, Angelo released her wrist. But he held his ground, his body blocking her path. "But it is—?"

Allison stepped to the side, determined to get by. Her fingers tightened around the leash, her nails digging into her palm. The nervousness spilled over into her stomach, making her wonder at it. It was broad daylight, there were people around and she could more than take care of herself. Besides, there was Fate at her side. What was there to be nervous about?

But the feeling didn't leave as she looked defiantly into his eyes. It intensified.

"Mine. Well, since you're none the worse for wear—" she began coolly in a dismissive voice as she moved around him.

Angelo stepped in front of her again, unwilling to let her go so easily. "Oh, but I am."

She looked him over suspiciously. There wasn't a single bruise or cut evident as far as she could see. "Where?"

"My heart." In one smooth, fluid movement Angelo linked his sun-bronzed fingers over hers and slid her hand over his chest, placing it over his heart.

Muscle. She felt only muscle. A good deal of it. The one he had her resting on was as hard as any of the concrete she had ever poured. And yet a flicker of desire went through her, just as it had when their bodies touched, as she felt the rhythmic beating of his heart. The quick tattoo matched her own.

She snatched away her hand as if she had touched fire. Next to her Fate growled low, sensing her distress, the sudden flare of fear that came over her, then was pushed back. Allison kept her expression bland, her voice cool. "I thought it was something serious."

Angelo was more concerned by her tone of voice than by the dog's growl. But not put off. There was suddenly too much at stake. "It is."

Allison began to walk away again. She'd given up the notion of jogging. But her gait was quick and determined. "Then see a doctor. You'll find one listed under psychiatrist in the Yellow Pages," she tossed over her shoulder. "Send me the bill."

He took advantage of the opening. "I would if I knew your name," he called after her.

Allison stopped and opened her mouth as she turned around, then shut it again. He'd almost gotten her that time. "That's listed in the Yellow Pages, too."

He took a step toward her. "Under?"

Allison resumed walking quickly. She said the first thing that came to mind. "Granite."

Angelo stopped, his hands on his hips. "As in heart of—?"

Her laughter floated back to him, but she never eased her pace. "Something like that." It wasn't the first time someone had said that to her. But she had come to terms with it. There were responsibilities to take care of that left no room for anything else, for any personal life.

She was running out of his life as quickly, as suddenly, as she had run in. And he didn't even know her name.

Angelo watched her go for a moment, then, giving in to an impulse, he followed her. She stepped up her pace, jogging another long block until she stopped beside a sleek-looking Mercedes sedan. Black, elegant. Even in jogging clothes she seemed well suited to it.

Unlocking the passenger side, she dropped the dog's leash. Fate ambled into the back, making himself as comfortable as possible in the limited space. From where Angelo stood the dog seemed to take up the full length of the back seat. The woman who had aroused Angelo's desire and fired his imagination allowed herself the luxury of a long sigh before she dropped into the driver's seat, pulling the door closed after her. A moment later the Mercedes drove away from the curb and disappeared down the winding street, leaving Angelo behind.

Angelo hurried back to his ground-floor apartment, repeating the license plate number of the Mercedes over and over to himself. He didn't mean for it to end here, not if he could help it.

Shad McClellan spun around on his heel as he heard the office door open and close behind him. "Where the hell have you been?" He had already asked Shirley three times if Angelo had called and left a message. He hadn't come in earlier today and he hadn't called, which wasn't like him. They had a meeting to get to in Costa Mesa, one that required traveling at speeds that were higher than the existing limits if they were to arrive in time.

If he heard the agitation in his foster brother's voice, Angelo gave no sign. Sitting down in the swivel chair before Shad's desk, he turned it until he was facing the younger man. "Meeting the woman of my dreams."

Shad pulled out an extra tie from the side desk drawer. Angelo didn't own a tie. He'd always said he didn't believe in them. Shad kept a couple in his desk for his brother in case of meetings. "Anyone I know?"

"No." Angelo accepted the tie Shad thrust toward him and mechanically began the distasteful job of knotting it. "Not even anyone I know."

Shadrach stopped shoving papers into his briefcase and eyed the man who'd been his brother and best friend for over twenty years. Angelo had been acting strangely for the past couple of weeks, and Shad was growing concerned.

"Angie, if for some reason we don't land this mall extension bid, I want you to go on a long vacation." He snapped the lid on his briefcase and picked out a jacket from his closet to go with Angelo's tie. He settled on the navy one. "Here."

"Stop worrying. You're beginning to sound like Ma." Angelo shrugged into the jacket. There was a company to run and people who were depending on them. He had to snap out of his mood. "If we don't land the bid—" he followed Shad down the hall to the parking lot as he straightened out the back of his collar "—there won't be any money to go on vacation with."

Shad tossed the briefcase into the back seat of the silvergray Jaguar. The car was his one extravagance. Not a practical automobile for a man with a wife and two children, he thought, even though J.T. had encouraged him to buy it. It was just one of the reasons he loved her. She understood. "In case you haven't noticed, the company is doing very well," Shad reminded him.

Angelo sat in the passenger seat. They always used Shad's car whenever they went anywhere. Driving relaxed Shad. Angelo believed in letting people do what they liked best. He stared out the window as they pulled out of the lot and melded into the street traffic. "Yeah, well—"

"You, however, are not." Shad glanced at Angelo's wide, rugged face before turning his attention to the road. It was a face that inspired confidence, Shad thought. An honest face. And, at the moment, a troubled face. "Want to talk about it?"

In all the years they had spent together there had never been secrets between the two men. At times words weren't even necessary to convey feelings. Now Angelo couldn't find the right ones to explain the strange restlessness that was taking over his waking thoughts and pushing its way into his dreams. Dreams where he was drifting aimlessly on an endless sea, alone, lost. "Ever wonder where your life is going, Shad?"

Angelo was too young for a midlife crisis, Shad thought. He wondered what had triggered this. He laughed easily, hoping to snap his brother out of whatever it was that was bothering him.

"I never have enough time to wonder." First there had been an endless shift from foster home to foster home. Shad had been too busy comforting Dottie, taking care of her. Then there had been the welcomed warmth of the Marino home where there had always been things for a young boy to do in order to show his appreciation for the love given him without strings. After he graduated high school at eighteen, the legal age where he was no longer considered a foster child, Shad had stayed on with the Marinos and helped build up the family business. Marriage had come after that, with a ready-made family. No, there had been no time to wonder where his life was going. It had just gone.

Angelo smiled, thinking of the way his brother's life had progressed. "No, I guess not. Not with Frankie and J.T. and the baby around."

They were closer than most natural brothers. Shad heard what wasn't being said. "But you do."

Angelo shrugged, awkward at the admission, however slight. "Every time Ma'd bug me about settling down, I always said I'd have time. It'd happen when it was supposed to." He gestured in frustration, his hands always a part of every statement. "But now you're married with a family and Dottie's married with a kid—"

Shad shifted lanes, preparing to take the off ramp. "Kids," he corrected. The road curved into almost a full circle before it fed into the street below.

Angelo forgot about his own concerns. He turned toward Shad, stunned. "You mean—?"

Shad's grin spread from ear to ear, matching the budding one on Angelo's face. "Yup."

"No kidding?" Memories of a pigtailed tomboy, sliding into third base and crashing into him, vividly rose up in his mind's eye. Dottie, pregnant. Happiness for his sister warred with his own feelings of being left out of life's mainstream.

The mall loomed ahead of them on the right and grew larger as they approached it. "She had to stop telling me about it to go lie down. She was afraid that her breakfast was going to make a second appearance." Turning the car to the right, Shad noticed the unguarded look on Angelo's face. It was nothing if not wistful. "What's the matter? Something wrong?"

Angelo shook his head. "No, nothing. I just want that too."

For once there was plenty of available parking. Shad found a spot near one of the mall's entrances. He stopped the car and then looked at Angelo, his hand still on the parking brake. "You want morning sickness?"

Angelo laughed as he got out. He looked over the roof of the car at his younger brother. "No, I just want everything that goes with it."

Walking through the entrance, they hurried to the offices located directly above the center of the mall. Angelo passed a woman pushing a stroller, and he felt that same wistful enviousness come over him. He had, he realized, a longing, a yen. His lips curved slightly. A baby yen. "And I don't know if it's going to happen for me, Shad. I want a wife, a baby, the whole American dream. I'm thirty-six years old—"

"And part owner of a hell of a construction company," Shad reminded him.

It wasn't enough. Gripping the railing on the up escalator, Angelo turned toward Shad. "There's got to be something else. It was enough when I was twenty-five, but it's not enough anymore. I want what Pop had, what you and Dottie have."

Shad stepped off behind Angelo, then turned toward the left. Angelo fell into step next to him. "So what's stopping you?" Shad had never thought about getting married until

it had happened. It had all fallen into place without calcu-
lation.

Angelo's wide shoulders rose and fell beneath his single-
breasted navy sport jacket. "I never saw anyone I thought
I wanted to spend forever with. Until today."

His hand raised to knock on the door that was all but
hidden, blending in with the rest of the mall's rustic decor.
Shad stopped and stared at Angelo. "You're serious?" It
had happened that quickly for him, too. He had taken one
look at J.T. and had known that this was different. It hadn't
taken much more time than that to realize that he wanted the
lady in his life permanently.

"Never more." Angelo sighed as the memory of the brief
encounter flashed through his mind. "She came up to my
shoulder." He touched it with his wide hand for emphasis
and grinned. "Five feet of blond dynamite being led around
by a dog."

The meeting forgotten for a moment, Shad leaned a
shoulder against the beige wall. "Come again?"

"She was jogging with a Great Dane and ran right into
me. Actually, over me."

Shad tried to picture it. "Will this get any clearer if you
repeat it?"

To talk about it somehow diminished a little of the magic.
And he wanted to savor it. Until he tracked her down.
"No."

Shad laughed. "I didn't think so. So what's her name?"

He hated admitting this. "I don't know. She wouldn't tell
me."

"Do you know anything about her at all?"

The grin grew wide again as Angelo remembered. "She
has great form when she jogs."

He had it bad, Shad thought with a shake of his head.
"That doesn't really help."

"And I've got the license number of her Mercedes."

Shad gave a low whistle. "At least when you fall, you fall for class." He straightened up. "We'll see about tracking down your mystery lady after our meeting with Walters." Shad knocked on the door and a sedate, officious-looking woman in her fifties opened the door almost immediately.

"Hello, gentlemen. He's been waiting for you." She turned and began leading them toward the back of the hall-way through a brightly lit corridor.

"So, Wanda, did we land the bid?" Angelo asked, easily reverting to the charm that caused everyone to like him al-most instantly.

The older woman looked at him, and the lines around her mouth and eyes seemed to vanish as she responded to his smile. "Looks that way to me." She winked broadly.

Angelo and Shad exchanged looks, pleased. Marino and McClellan had come a long way from the days when it was simply Marino's. Then it had been a tile company. Salvator Marino had kept the nature of his business restricted to bathroom renovations. It had taken Shad with his inherent skill, enthusiasm and natural drive to broaden the base of the company.

Salvator had taken Shad and Dottie in and had become, for all intents and purposes, their father. Unable to adopt them legally because of a technicality, Salvator and Bridg-ette Marino had adopted the two abandoned orphans in all other aspects. So much so that there was no difference be-tween the way Angelo, Shad and Dottie regarded one an-other when they were growing up. They were siblings and the Marino house was home to all of them.

But Shad had a family now, a fifteen-year-old stepson as well as a new baby. It wouldn't be fair to them to have Shad put in the kind of hours he had before he was married. Fif-teen- or twenty-hour days were all right if there was no one home waiting for you. And for Angelo there wasn't. The fact had never bothered him until just recently. In the past year he'd changed his mind about the warmth and affection that was evident at the perennial Sunday dinners his mother liked to preside over. He was part of all that, part of each of the separate nuclei and part of the whole they created. And yet he was alone, apart from it. Shad and his family and Dottie and hers came faithfully each Sunday. And there was always an extra chair for anyone Angelo chose to bring. But it was rarely filled. There was no one he cared enough about to bring to one of those dinners.

He had begun to wonder if there ever would be.

As they approached the door to the inner office at the end of the hall, Angelo shook off his depression. The company he and Shad had carefully nurtured had already built one mini-mall in Malibu and had a hand in the construction of several others. They were coming up in the world, and this was no time to mourn over things that weren't going right in his life. He had always been one to count his blessings. It was his nature to see the possibilities instead of the obstacles.

Shad couldn't ignore the concern he felt over Angelo's mood. It transcended any contract they hoped to win. Angelo was far more important to him than any business deal. He stopped just before entering the office. "Listen, Angie, if you don't feel like sitting in, I can—"

"What, and have you hog all the glory? No way. Hey, I'm fine, really." Angelo's smile returned, his dark eyes flashing with that infectious zest for life he always retained, even in the darkest moments. What was to be, would be. It was the first lesson his father had taught him. It had rung true then and it would now. "C'mon, Shad." He threw his arm casually around Shad's shoulder. "Let's snare our next piece of the great American dream while it's still hot."

They followed Wanda inside the office.

The main office of Montgomery and Walters, the firm that oversaw everything that went on within the Southern California Mall, was large but subdued, a testimony to Adrian Walters's good taste. A thin, diminutive man, Walters stood rather than sat behind his desk, ready to greet the two men he was awaiting. Three wing chairs faced his desk. And it looked as if someone was occupying the one farthest from the door.

With the chair turned sideways, all Angelo saw were long, slender legs.

"Ah, it's late. We were just about to start," Walters said, extending his hand to Shad and then Angelo.

"We?" Shad looked over toward the occupied chair.

"Yes." Walters nodded at the person sitting in the chair on his left.

Rising, the woman turned around and looked at the two men. Her expression remained the same, but her eyes widened slightly in recognition and surprise.

Angelo was never one for such subtle gestures. His mouth dropped open as he looked at the woman who had jogged over his heart.

Chapter Two

In thirty-six years Angelo couldn't remember a single time he had been at a loss for words, not even the time the vice principal had caught him and four other boys carrying a table out of the cafeteria. His glib tongue and quick mind had been fast enough to enable him to talk his way out of the harmless prank. All words seemed momentarily to escape him now.

Shad pulled him over by his arm. "What's the matter?" he whispered. "You look as if you've seen a ghost."

Angelo shook his head slowly, his eyes never leaving the woman's face. "Not a ghost." He smiled at her. "My future."

She drew her breath in sharply. Who was this man? Allison threw a quizzical look toward Walters, hoping against hope that somehow this was all a mistake. These men had to be at the wrong meeting. Maybe they were supposed to be next door at the Universal Toy Shoppe.

Angelo had received a blow to the head on their last construction job. Neither one of them had thought it was anything serious then. Now Shad wasn't so sure. He pressed his lips together and looked from Angelo to the woman in the room. What the hell was going on?

Angelo crossed the room to her. Allison suddenly felt as if the dark rich mahogany paneling was closing in on her, making it difficult to breathe. He put out his hand to her. "Angelo Marino. Looks like we meet sooner than you would have expected."

Allison could see by Walters's expression that these men hadn't stumbled into the wrong meeting. They were supposed to be here. She had no choice but to accept Angelo's extended hand. She didn't want to take it. She didn't want any contact with the man. There had already been too much to suit her. "This is sooner than never, yes," she responded icily, hoping that would put him off.

So this was the woman with the romping Great Dane whom Angelo had been so moonstruck about, Shad thought. Taking a closer look he could see why. The lady had very nice lines. "I can see you really made a good impression on her," Shad murmured to his brother.

Angelo grinned, still holding the hand that had long since purposely gone limp in his. "No, she made one on me. Actually, her dog did." He glanced toward Walters. "Right here." Angelo tapped his chest.

Walters looked at the threesome, confused. "You all know one another, then?"

"No," Angelo and Allison chorused in unison.

The way Angelo looked at her annoyed Allison. It was entirely too intimate, too personal. Just because their bodies had accidentally tangled for a minute didn't give him the right to look at her with the kind of familiarity she felt was reserved only for lovers.

And why were these two men here to begin with? She had thought the bid had been won by her company. "I have no idea who he is," Allison informed Walters. "And I—"

She got no further as the door behind Shad and Angelo cracked open slightly and Wanda stuck her head in. Allison noticed that she smiled at Angelo before she addressed Walters. "I'm very sorry to interrupt, Mr. Walters, but the people about the carousel are here."

Walters ran two fingers over his very trim mustache. "I'm in a meeting, Wanda," he pointed out. Signs of stress were becoming visible.

The older woman nodded patiently. "I'm aware of that, sir. They promised to take only a moment of your time. It's about the color scheme being changed."

"Why does everything come due when Montgomery is on vacation?" Walters closed his eyes as if he were searching for some inner solace that wasn't forthcoming. When he opened them again, he looked at the three people in front of his desk, then lifted his lips in a smile that could have been drawn in place for all the emotion that was behind it.

"I'll be right back, " he promised, moving to the door. "Since the three of you are all in construction, I'm sure you'll find something to talk about." With a fussy little movement he eased the door shut behind him.

Angelo looked at the woman next to him. She was dressed in an almost mannish beige business suit. He liked the jogging outfit better.

"You're in construction?" He found it difficult to believe that someone so delicate-looking could have anything to do with the construction industry. Maybe she was a secretary sent to take an order for supplies once they got the operation off the ground. But even as he thought of the idea, he dismissed it. He and Shad had their own list of suppliers and subcontractors they dealt with. Walters had nothing to do with that end of it.

She didn't care for his tone. It was too incredulous. He sounded as if he was laughing at her. "Yes, I am."

Her tone begged for the statement to be ended with "You wanna make something of it?" Getting information from her was like pulling teeth. Very pretty, evenly shaped teeth, he noticed, his eyes dipping to her mouth. Big mistake, he thought, sensations rising up through him. He remembered that mouth being only inches from his, and a dull ache came over him. He had been slow then. He promised himself not to be slow the next time the opportunity presented itself. And it would. "And you represent—?"

She kept her eyes straight ahead, wishing that Walters would hurry up. She wanted to get this over with. Outside, she knew it was another perfect Southern California day. In here there was only furniture and bookshelves. And a very nosy man. She had completely forgotten about Angelo's partner. "Conrad and Son."

She said it as if she was proclaiming royal bloodlines. He'd heard of the company. Who hadn't? The firm had been around for a long time and was responsible for some of Orange County's finest structures. Angelo cocked his head and grinned. "Which one are you?"

She drew her shoulders up as she sat straighter in her chair. "I'm the Son."

He was being flippant. Actually he hadn't expected her to be either one. "There's an explanation that goes with this, right?"

Reluctantly Allison put out her hand. "Allison Conrad. My father is responsible for the company's name. He calls me Sonny."

Maybe his high opinion of the firm should be reevaluated. "He wears glasses, I take it."

Allison thought of her father, a sharp-featured, handsome man, his face pulled into a frown as he scanned reports she gave him. Crystal-blue eyes looking at her disapprovingly through thick lenses. "As a matter of fact, yes."

How anyone could even remotely apply the title "Sonny" to a woman who looked so sensually feminine was beyond him. "Give me a list of the buildings you've worked on and I'll make a note to stay clear of them."

It was a joke wrapped in a compliment, but he could see that she didn't take it that way. For the first time in his life Angelo felt as if he was floundering.

The big oaf. Did he think she'd be flattered if he ran down her father's work? And didn't he realize that she'd be involved in each building, as well? "No need," she told him coldly. "We only use the finest materials. I'll back every one of our constructions."

Angelo retreated for a moment. "I'll keep that in mind."

She found being blunt was best with certain types of people. "Try keeping a professional attitude in mind, as well."

Shad wondered what had come over Angelo. He'd never seen him tripping over his own tongue this way. Well, maybe things would level off now that it seemed she'd put him in his place. Angelo's next question, coming out of the blue, told Shad he'd guessed wrong.

"Are you married?"

Allison's eyes widened in surprise, then narrowed at the question. Now he was digging into her personal life. Just who the hell did he think he was? "No."

That was good. Angelo leaned closer. "Spoken for?" he prodded despite Shad's firm tug on his elbow.

She'd had just about enough. "No one speaks for me." It was something she'd yet to make her father understand. He saw her only as an appendage. One who, she knew, continued to disappoint him.

"They probably wouldn't dare," Shad murmured under his breath. When Allison's sharp blue eyes turned his way, Shad flashed a quick smile and leaned past Angelo. "Shad McClellan. The silent partner."

He nodded at Angelo and retreated back to his observations. This was something new. Angelo was usually rather laid-back when it came to women. As long as Shad could remember, it had always been a matter of his foster brother being oblivious to the feminine attention he garnered. There had never been a serious romance for him, just a parade of lively, attractive women passing through his life. To the woeful despair of Mama Marino, Angelo had been disinterested in settling down and totally immune to the advances of any one of a number of women who would have been more than willing to bear Angelo's name and his children.

Until, apparently, now.

Shad leaned back in his chair and unobtrusively studied the woman who had so obviously caught his brother's fancy. Small, neatly dressed in a sand-colored two-piece suit made of some expensive fabric he didn't know the name of, Shad noted that she didn't have a single hair out of place. It was neatly pulled back, not to accentuate her amazing cheekbones—but because it was obviously more efficient that way. It wouldn't get in her way. She looked like a lady who valued efficiency and who didn't let *anything* get in her way.

He couldn't help wondering if Angelo detected the stubborn, independent streak that he saw. Probably not. Angelo went for the big picture every time. Shad had always been the one who saw to the minutiae that was involved in their work.

He also wondered if she was good enough for Angelo. There were very few women, in Shad's estimation, who were. Angelo Marino, like his father before him, was a very special man with a heart that was a lot larger than any heart had a right to be.

Shad hoped it wasn't about to get trampled on.

Suppressing a sigh, Shad shifted in his chair and looked toward the door, hoping Walters would get back soon before any fireworks began next to him. Angelo was old enough to take care of himself. Shad only hoped that he could remember that and stay out of it. He knew that Dottie wouldn't. Things like common sense and privacy had never stopped his sister before. Of the three of them, she'd always been the one to rush in where angels feared to tread. Shad glanced from Angelo to Allison.

Until now, he amended.

Allison felt herself fidgeting inside. She *hated* fidgeting. Why should the way this man looked at her, as if he knew something about her that she didn't, make her feel fidgety? It was ridiculous. Yet she did. "Mr. Marino," she began, hoping for some professional footing to offset the way she felt, "I have no idea why we're all here—"

"Maybe it has something to do with the mall addition," Angelo suggested, humor lifting the corners of his generous mouth.

He was patronizing her. She might have known. He was the type. She was used to boors, to men who liked to throw their weight around women and belittle them. She'd been in their midst most of her life, showing them that they were wrong, that she could be every bit as good as a man. Showing her father that she was every bit as good as a man. She'd spent her whole life proving that to him. Or trying to.

Her mouth hardened slightly. "I'm sure it does. What I meant is I don't know what you're doing here. I was given to understand that the job was being awarded to Conrad and Son."

"Well, unless we're being awarded to Conrad and Son, as well," Angelo said, amused, "this might be about something else."

She was a little high and mighty, he thought. But he had come to know at an early age that that kind of behavior was usually a defense mechanism, a shield thrown up and meant to protect a raw vulnerability behind it. Shad had been like that when he first came to live with them. A brazen little tough guy who was afraid to reach out and love because of all the rejection he had suffered. Angelo had a suspicion he was encountering the same thing again in Allison.

Except that she was a hell of a lot prettier than Shad had ever been.

The sound of the door being opened again had all three of them turning. Angelo saw relief flash in Allison's eyes, although she was probably unaware of it. He wondered what it would be like to see something else flash there instead, something far more personal.

"Sorry to keep you all waiting," Walters said, hurrying back to his desk. "There doesn't seem to be a free moment anymore." He glanced in Allison's direction for sympathy and received none. Clearing his throat a little self-consciously, he got to the business at hand. "Well, it seems that you both submitted the exact same bid."

Allison turned toward Angelo. Her look was nothing short of accusing. It amused Angelo rather than provoked him. He leaned over and whispered, "We didn't peek, honest."

There wasn't a single thing about this man's attitude that she liked. It was entirely too unprofessional and whimsical. He probably thought that competing with her company was just a big joke. Well, he was in for a surprise. "Then we'll just submit another one," she told Walters, ignoring Angelo.

Walters sat back and steepled his fingers thoughtfully. "I don't see the need to continue that way. I thought perhaps, since the job is so large, it could be split between the two firms. I've talked to my associates and they've agreed." He dropped his hands and sat forward, more intent. "It would get built faster that way."

"Like the two railroads starting from opposite ends of the country and meeting in the middle," Angelo said, watching Walters's face. It had been Frankie's history lesson yesterday, and he had made a point to help his nephew with the boy's weakest subject.

Walters nodded vigorously, pleased. "Yes, something like that." He paused, then rushed through the rest of his words. "If you split the bid in half—"

Allison rose before Walters was finished. "That's not acceptable." It was an insult to expect her company to work with another company. They had always done the job alone.

"Half of something is better than all of nothing," Angelo said softly, repeating one of his father's favorite axioms.

Walters shifted his gaze to Angelo. "I do like the way you think, Mr. Marino."

Angelo smiled easily, his deep green eyes lazily coming to rest on the other man's eager face. He knew exactly what the man was up to. He intended to go him one better. It served his purpose to agree to this.

"But perhaps you could think a little larger, Mr. Walters," he suggested. He saw a nervous frown twitch the man's lips. "Say, perhaps, five-eighths the fee for each company?"

Shad sat back, content to let Angelo run the negotiations for a change. He rather liked this side of his brother. It rarely surfaced. Love did strange things to a man, he mused.

Walters frowned more deeply as he pulled at the point of his chin. "That doesn't add up to a whole."

"No," Angelo agreed. "But it does add up to getting the extension done faster. That was your point." He leaned forward, keeping his eyes on Walters, trying his damnedest to blot out the flowery scent spilling through his senses as it drifted over from Allison. "Customers brought in quicker. What do you say?"

It was clear that Walters was torn between saving a sizable amount of money and having stores ready to do business that much earlier. The mall would be increased by over one-third its size. More stores always brought in more people. Angelo watched as Walters weighed time versus money. In the long run added customers would more than make up for the initial outlay. "All right, we'll do it your way."

It was still a man's world, just as it always had been. And she was going to have to continue poking holes into it if she was ever to get any breathing space. "Their way, Mr. Walters," she corrected.

The three men turned to look at her, as if suddenly remembering she was in the room. That was only true of Walters. Shad and Angelo had never forgotten.

A delicate hand, more suited to playing piano than to construction work, waved in the direction of the two men who were clearly her competitors. "Conrad and Son hasn't agreed to anything." She expected Walters to reconsider his stand. Her father wouldn't approve of the way things were going if she returned to him with this proposition.

Small black eyes darted from Angelo's face to Allison's and then back again. "If you wish to pull out, Ms. Conrad, then you'll leave me no choice but to go with Marino and McClellan—"

"And revert back to the initial bid," Shad quickly put in.

Walters bobbed his head twice. "Yes, of course."

She was going to lose the bid. Damn that man, anyway, she thought, leveling an accusing glance at Angelo. She hadn't a single leg to stand on if she wanted to secure the mall extension exclusively for her company. She held back a sigh.

It wasn't that Conrad and Son needed the job. They were well established, had been for over thirty-five years. But she needed to win this bid. If she returned and told her father that the bid was lost, he'd look at her in that way that always told her he wished he had had a son to carry on instead of her. She hated that look, had done everything in her power to blot it out. And the words that it always carried with it, words that echoed in her head long after the sounds of the day had died away: "If it weren't for you—"

It always came down to that. If it weren't for her.

Allison slowly took her seat. She remained on the edge of it, Angelo noted, as if she couldn't relax, didn't know how to relax. He was going to enjoy teaching her.

"I didn't say we wouldn't do it."

Walters blinked, clearly not following her. "Just what is it that you did say, Ms. Conrad?"

She addressed her words to Walters, but her eyes were on Angelo, daring him to take exception. "That we'll split this job on an equal basis."

"Of course," Walters agreed quickly.

She shifted, looking now at Shad. Her glance took in the thin gold band on his left hand. If she had to trust anyone in this partnership, she had a feeling it would be him. "And no independent decisions will be made. If there's something to be done, to be decided on, we'll all be involved in the negotiations. I intend to be on the job every day." It was said to show Angelo how serious she was about this. She was a hands-on engineer.

Angelo crossed one ankle over his thigh and grinned engagingly. "I'm looking forward to working with you."

Allison ignored him. She could do that for now. But she had a feeling that it wasn't going to be easy to ignore him in the months of work that lay ahead. He didn't strike her as the type that would stay ignored willingly. Well, she could handle that. She'd handled it before. She didn't need some macho man in a tool belt messing up her life. She'd been around construction workers all her life and knew how to avoid the "Me Tarzan, You Jane" situation. Besides, she took pride in her work and let nothing get in the way. She took her responsibilities seriously. It was all she had.

That settled, Walters unfurled the drawing of the architect's conceptualization of the mall's extension. It covered his entire desk.

"We're going to call it the Emerald Plaza." With the tip of his pencil he indicated the huge three-story dome that was the focal point of the entire extension. The stories jutted out in three separate directions on two levels. The fourth direction was where the extension fed into the existing mall.

They had all seen the drawing before when they placed their bids. But now it was theirs to build and the feeling was somehow different, more personal. Perhaps too personal.

Allison realized that Angelo was standing next to her. She was tempted to move aside, but stayed where she was. It was the best way to deal with someone like him. She couldn't let him know that he was getting to her in any manner.

"I would like the ground-breaking to get under way as soon as possible," Walters told them. "Say, next week?"

He and Shad had already discussed this. "We can have our people here by Monday," Angelo told Walters. Then he looked at Allison. "If that's all right with you."

She didn't know if he was patronizing her or playing according to the rules. She relaxed only fractionally. Life had taught her that. If you relaxed, things rolled right over you. "That's all right with me. I can have a crew ready by seven."

"Eight?" Angelo suggested.

He'd be the type who liked to sleep in, she thought. Maybe he wouldn't show up at all, just have his partner run the show at the site. "Like to stay in bed?" It was meant to be a criticism.

His eyes swept over her. "If the occasion is right."

The smile was lazy and all the more sexy for it. Allison bit her lower lip in frustration. How could she be reacting to such an annoying man?

"Actually," Shad interrupted quickly, putting himself physically between Angelo and Allison, "we were thinking that seven might be a little too early to start working. This is a residential area and seven is kind of early to put up with the jarring sound of bulldozers."

He looked at Allison, waiting for her to agree. Shad had a feeling that his main function on this job was going to be that of perennial peacemaker. The thought made him grin. Wait until he got home and told the family that love had finally found Angelo Marino. Mama was going to be overjoyed. In his heart he sincerely doubted that Allison stood a chance.

Allison drew herself up to her full height. She realized that she was rubbing her thumb against her index finger. It was a nervous habit she had had since she was a child. How many times had she stood fidgeting that way before her father when she was growing up? Too many. She pushed the thought away.

She deliberately picked up her briefcase and held on to it, immobilizing her hand. "All right, the crew can begin at eight o'clock." She turned to Angelo, her face somber. "But I'd like to meet with you at the site at seven-thirty Monday morning. Sharp."

"Pistols at ten paces?" Angelo guessed, reading the look in her eyes. Why did she feel the need to see them as a personal threat? he wondered. And what would it take to get her to trust them? To trust him?

For a second Allison relished the idea of an old-fashioned duel, with herself as the victor. Too bad things were more civilized these days.

"That choice, Mr. Marino, is yours. I just thought it'd be a good time to get some ground rules cleared up." She looked at Shad expectantly. Of the two, she figured him to be the saner one. There wasn't a strange gleam in his eye when he looked at her.

"Fine with me," Shad answered.

She tucked the briefcase under her arm. "Here's my card." She deliberately gave it to Shad and not Angelo. "Call me if there's a change in your plans. Otherwise I'll see you then."

Angelo held the door for her as she nodded goodbye to Walters. "Count on it," Angelo assured her departing back. Allison didn't bother to turn around. The sound of her heels echoed down the long hallway.

Angelo began whistling as soon as the door closed behind them.

"You like doing things the hard way, don't you?" Shad asked, thinking of Allison. He'd never met a woman more inclined to resist the attentions of a man. Except, perhaps, for J.T. Initially. But then that had been part of the attraction.

Angelo pulled off his tie with a grateful flourish and stuck it into the pocket of his jacket. He sighed with relief as he opened up the two top buttons and then took a deep breath. Formality always seemed to cut off his air supply. "I've always loved a challenge."

Angelo had always been one who naturally found and used the easy way out. "Since when?" Shad laughed.

Angelo checked his watch, then looked up and grinned at Shad. "Oh, since just a little more than two and a half hours ago."

Chapter Three

It took Allison over thirty-five minutes to drive back to the spacious fourth-floor offices Conrad and Son occupied on Newport Center Drive.

The offices were laid out so that they had a sumptuous view of the Pacific. Not that her father ever looked out. She seriously doubted Miles Conrad even knew the ocean existed just beyond his window. After all, he hadn't had a hand in constructing it. God's architecture didn't interest Miles Conrad. Only his own.

She parked her car in the covered structure beneath her office building, lining the black sedan up neatly in front of her name. Traffic had been heavy for midafternoon and the trip had taken her fifteen minutes longer than usual. But the extra fifteen minutes hadn't been enough time for her to find the right words to inform her father of the new twist. She was just going to have to be blunt and say it outright. Allison anticipated his reaction with a surge of dread.

She walked into the outer office and nodded at the duo of secretaries before her father's door.

"How did it go, Sonny?" Tracy, the younger of the two secretaries, asked.

"It went." Allison frowned as she looked toward her father's office door. "Is he in?"

Phyllis, her father's secretary for over twenty years, nodded. "He's waiting for you."

Allison knew he would be. She was just taking a few extra seconds to fortify herself for the ordeal ahead. She loved her father but hated to deal with him. She ran her thumb over her forefinger, then clenched her hands at her sides. Stupid to have jitters walking in to talk to your own father. Even if he was your boss.

It was like preparing for a visit to the dentist. Except that she had to endure it a lot more often than every six months. Blowing out a breath, Allison pulled back her shoulders, unconsciously bracing herself the way she always did whenever she was about to see her father. She knocked briskly, then opened the door and walked in.

Miles Conrad was seated at his desk, his attention focused on his work. Unlike the men who worked for him, Miles totally eschewed using a computer. That was what his secretaries were for. His notes were all written in longhand, the letters tight and precise. At least the accident hadn't taken the use of his hands away from him.

He always knew just how to deliver a wound, she thought, watching him now.

Allison stood in the doorway and waited. Her first memory of her father was seeing him in this office. She had been about three. Her mother had taken her to eat at a restaurant that had clowns painted on the walls and they had stopped by afterward. Despite her mother's chidings, Allison had run in, excited to see her father. He hadn't looked up when she entered the office then, either. She crossed her arms. Some things never changed, she thought. Her lips twisted into an ironic smile.

Several minutes dragged by. He knew she was standing there. He was doing this intentionally. She wondered why being a tyrant gave him such pleasure.

Miles placed his fountain pen on the desk and pushed his thick glasses up the bridge of his perfectly shaped nose. He had always been a handsome man. She supposed that was what had attracted her mother to him in the first place. But handsome only went so far. "You're late."

She took that as her invitation to come in and sit down. She perched rather than sat, although she did it displaying a certain degree of self-assurance. She was good at playing the part after all these years. Since her mother had died, she hadn't felt comfortable in her father's presence, yet she refused to let him see her uneasiness. It would have been too great a victory for him. "Traffic was heavy."

His voice was low, cultured. Emotionless. "You should have allowed for it."

She saw a letter from the Shirrell Corporation on his desk. Idly she touched a corner and moved it slightly in her direction. She wondered if the hotel chain was expanding again. Conrad and Son had handled their last three new hotels. "I did."

He raised his eyes slowly to her face, the judge listening to the accused before sentence was passed. He turned the letter back toward him. "What happened?"

Her slim shoulders rose and fell beneath her tailored jacket. "My allowance fell short."

The expression on his face told her he would have expected as much from her. He always looked at her that way. The years had only intensified it. It still rankled her.

By now, she chided herself, she should have grown immune to it. Superficially she had. Allison prided herself on keeping her reaction to her father's slights bottled up, out of sight. But deep inside, where she lived, it stung. It always stung.

A grown woman of twenty-nine shouldn't be hung up on getting her father's approval. She had reprimanded herself for that attitude time and again. Yet here she was with those same feelings coursing through her. Perhaps his approval wouldn't have meant so much if she had had it at least once.

But Miles Conrad had never been one to give praise freely to anyone, least of all her. He had always been a perfectionist. He demanded nothing less of himself, nothing less of those who worked for him. If it was delivered, he was satisfied, taking it as his due. When it wasn't, there was hell to pay. Since he had been trapped in a wheelchair, he had gotten worse.

Miles studied his only daughter closely. Impatience flickered in his steel-blue eyes. The glasses only magnified it. "So are you going to tell me how it went, or do I have to make a formal request in writing?"

She was tempted to look away, but that would have been the coward's way out. And she had never been a coward, although she guessed that her father would have probably preferred her to be. "We break ground on the project next Monday."

His eyes narrowed, drawing the truth from her. "Then the bid was satisfactory?"

She rose, knowing she would begin fidgeting if she didn't. "Obviously. So satisfactory that it turned up twice."

There was a fresh pot of tea by his desk. Phyllis saw to it three times daily. It was one of the things he insisted on. One of the many. He raised the delicate china cup to his lips now and sipped, his eyes on her. He set it down again with a clatter. "What are you babbling about?"

Allison drew herself up to her full height, then felt a flash of guilt when she saw the look on her father's face. She had legs and could stand and he couldn't. And it was her fault. She sat again. "I am not babbling, Father. I'm trying to find the right words to tell you that we're not handling the mall extension by ourselves."

"Oh?"

The single word was encrusted with ice. Damn, she wasn't five anymore. She was twenty-nine. She had graduated at the top of her class in engineering—just to show him because he had said she didn't have what it took. She had been able to build things and cut through problems that stood in her way since she could walk. Why did she always feel so incompetent around her father, as if tying her shoes was too taxing a proposition?

Because he wanted her to feel that way. It gave him control over her. And because she felt responsible for his being in a wheelchair, she let him.

There was no point in going over it again. It was all a given. She addressed the problem at hand and blocked out everything else. "It seems that Marino and McClellan handed in the same bid." She had been the one to prepare the bid. He was going to blame her for this, as he did for everything else that went wrong.

"Marino and McClellan?" Miles echoed as if he were reciting the names found on the label of a can of inexpensive dog food. "That sounds like a second-rate comedy team."

Annoyance built at his disparaging comment. He knew nothing about them. How could he just cut people down like that, dismiss their worth with a wave of his hand? With an uncalled-for remark? She knew the answer to that. Easily. She had watched him do it all of her life. "There's nothing second-rate about them. They happen to be very competent general contractors." She had no idea what possessed her to say that. Anger at her father's assumption, she supposed.

He raised a brow as he steepled his fingers. He took contradiction very badly, but he was willing to listen if it was dressed in the truth. "You've seen their work?"

Her father saw through lies. Allison took her chances. She was out on a limb as it was. Her eyes never wavered from his. "Yes."

"I see." He pushed his wheelchair back slightly, away from the desk. The chair was the latest in mobile technology, built like a sleek black office chair that tilted and swiveled at the touch of his hand, adjusting to his every whim. He hated it, Allison knew.

"Make up a list for me. I want to see some examples of their work for myself."

"I'll get on it right away." She'd have to get the list from Marino. That meant calling him. She rubbed her thumb over her forefinger.

Miles's displeasure at the arrangement was obvious. "I don't like having my reputation tied up with someone else's."

After seven years with the company, it was still "my," not "our." She was knocking her head against a stone wall. "I know that, but it can't be helped this time, not if we want a hand in the project." She knew prestige was still important to him. It always had been.

He adjusted his chair so that he tilted back. "So what are the arrangements?"

Details were what she was good at. They gave her leverage. "We work together on the job, split it fifty-fifty. No decisions are made about anything without all parties being consulted."

"I don't like anyone looking over my shoulder." He let out an annoyed huff.

"Technically it'll be my shoulder," Allison pointed out. And she didn't relish the idea of having Marino there, day in, day out. She hardly thought, after their initial meeting in Walters's office, that Marino would stay on his own side unless there was a meeting. He was going to be underfoot and she knew it.

"Same thing," Miles reminded her tersely. He took another sip of his tea, then warmed it by adding more from the china pot. "And the money?"

"Both companies get five-eighths of the bid." She watched his face. Money always appealed to him.

He looked surprised. More than half the money for half the work. "Your idea?"

She would have liked to have taken the credit just to see what he'd say. But she had already fudged one answer. She wasn't about to make a habit of it, even academically. "Angelo thought of that."

Funny how easily the man's name came to her lips. He was an annoying, muscle-bound oaf who was probably going to give her more than her share of headaches on this project with what he probably viewed to be his charming manner. Yet when her father criticized him, something had made her want to ride to the rescue. Rebellion, she supposed. It certainly didn't have anything to do with the man himself.

Miles tugged his glasses off to glare at her. "Angelo? Who the hell is Angelo?"

"Angelo Marino," she clarified. "His partner's name is Shad McClellan."

"You sound like you know him personally," he said suspiciously.

She saw the look in her father's eyes. He probably thought he smelled a conspiracy. It angered her beyond words that he could think that way about her. "No, but I intend to. One should always know one's competition." She rose, picking up her briefcase. She had work to see to and it wouldn't get done in here. "You taught me that."

"Surprised you remembered."

"I remember everything." Allison looked at him pointedly.

He obviously chose to see no hidden message in her words. "See that you do." Allison saw the wheels turning in his head. "Five-eighths?"

"Yes."

"What about the penalty clause if we don't do each phase on time?"

"It's still the same." She knew what he was thinking. This was a joint venture now and they sank or swam together. The penalty was steep. It had been included out of pride. Now the terms had been altered. More people were involved. And a chain was only as strong as its weakest link.

He shook his head. Not a single silver hair on his head fell out of place. It probably didn't dare, she thought. "It's lucky I built up this company to be financially solvent. Left in your hands we'd be in ruins in a matter of months."

Enough was enough. "Five-eighths of the bid for half the work isn't going to reduce us to paupers, Father. *Forbes* magazine doesn't list the leading paupers in the country on their pages," she reminded him archly.

Her grandfather had started the company, bringing in her father and uncle when it was time. Together they had built it up to be the hugely successful and renowned company it was today. Her grandfather had died at his desk, working. He had suffered a major heart attack, ignoring the telltale signs of impending disaster until it was too late. Her uncle had retired then, determined to enjoy his own life before it was too late. Her father had taken three hours off for the funeral before returning to the office and the current project. She had wondered how he had managed to work the funeral into his schedule.

Miles disliked flippancy. "You always did have a smart mouth."

She didn't bother pretending to smile. "Goes with the brains, Father, both of which I inherited from you."

The heart, Allison added silently, *I got from Mother.*

God, she missed her mother, even after all these years. Margaret Conrad had died when Allison was only five. She lived on in Allison's mind, enshrined in bits and pieces of deeply treasured memories. The smell of lilacs in springtime. A warm hug by a cheery fireplace. A gentle hand brushing her hair. Soft, melodic laughter that seemed to fill a field of wildflowers. Everything that was warm and precious, that was her mother. It wasn't pneumonia that had taken her mother from her. Allison strongly suspected that Margaret Conrad had withered away from lack of love and attention. Few things grew, much less thrived, in earth that was as hard as her father's heart.

That was why, when she was alone with her thoughts at the end of the day, she wondered why she tried so hard to reach it. Part of it, she supposed, was due to a child's longing. Every child wanted to be accepted by his parent to some degree.

The rest was guilt. He saw to that. If by some miracle there was no veiled reference to his activities being cut short by the accident, there was always the wheelchair to remind her of it. To remind her of that night almost five years ago when she decided to tell him that she was finally through trying to please him. That the education, the fight to get into his company, the constant fending off of cryptic, stinging remarks had made her tired and she was finally throwing in the towel. Her suitcase was in the trunk of her car, packed. Her life planned in another direction. She had the letter of acceptance from Taylor and Wells in her purse. She was going to join a construction firm in Nevada. The housing industry had begun to flourish there and there was the need for talented builders with engineering degrees.

A fresh start, away from her father, that had been her goal. She wanted a life of her own and she wanted it away from his shadow. Away from his perpetual frown that always found her lacking.

She had booked a flight out of LAX. All that remained was to tell him. She had put it off to the end, not wanting a long, drawn-out scene. Not wanting to give him the opportunity to go on for days about her lack of gratitude for all that he had done for her. Or to listen to his accusations of stealing clients. That would have been there, too.

She had volunteered to drive him to his meeting at the Sheridan Hotel. It had begun raining hard, a sudden June shower coming out of nowhere. She remembered carefully searching for the words to her declaration of independence. When they came she never got a chance to deliver them.

A van on the other side of the road jumped the divider and although she swerved to avoid it, it had rammed right into them. The last thing she remembered was screaming out her father's name.

Her father remained in a coma for two weeks. She had spent every minute at his side, refusing to leave. She had held his hand, talking to him as if he were alert, telling him about projects, desperately trying to keep him tethered to life. After two weeks, he awoke, as if coming out of a nightmare. Always an active man who'd prided himself on his physical prowess, he was horrified and enraged to discover that he was paralyzed from the waist down.

Allison had escaped the accident with only bruises and contusions. That was physically. Mentally it was another story. She was shackled. If she hadn't already blamed herself for the accident, her father was there to do it for her. Vaguely indifferent to her before, now he was bitter and caustically critical of everything she did, every decision she made both personally and professionally. She learned to live with it, to shut it out when it got too bad, to tolerate it and see it for what it was.

She had to be his legs, he had informed her while still in the hospital. He took her obedience for granted. No one had ever opposed him, so he hadn't expected things to be any different now. Especially not now. She wasn't the best qualified for the position, of course, he went on to say, staring at her over his atrophied limbs in the hospital bed, but blood counted for something, and since he had no son, she would have to do.

She stayed because it was her duty and she had been raised to respect that.

"Better put some of those brains you're boasting about to work." Miles picked up his fountain pen again. "You've wasted half the day already."

She bit back a retort. There was no use in telling him that she had sandwiched in only an hour this morning to jog between being at the office at six and going to the meeting with Walters about the mall extension. She put in more hours than anyone else at the company, except perhaps for him. But too much was never enough for him. It never would be.

Allison turned to go without a word in her own defense. She wouldn't give him the satisfaction.

Her father's voice followed her to the door. "I'll see you at dinner?"

She stopped, her hand on the doorknob, but she didn't turn around. "Of course."

After the accident, she had moved back home to help Edna, their housekeeper, care for her father while he was convalescing. Once he improved, Miles told Allison that there was no reason for her to move out again. It seemed logical enough to her at the time, especially since she had given up her apartment when she decided to move to Nevada. There was no reason to look for another apartment. Home was just a place to sleep at best. Her life now belonged to her father. It was a matter of atonement.

She took a deep breath, feeling better now that she was out of his office. She hurried to her own. He'd want that list before the end of the day. Before the end of the hour if she knew him. He wasn't one to let things slide. Allison stopped at her secretary's desk.

"Rhonda, get me the number for Marino and McClellan. It's a construction firm." She glanced at her watch and started toward her office. No time to go out to eat. She'd order a roast beef sandwich to be sent in.

"It might be on the card."

Allison stopped just a few steps shy of her office. "What card?"

"The card with the flowers." Rhonda, a romantic to the tips of her red hair, grinned broadly. "I peeked." Her bright green eyes egged Allison on for whatever details she might be willing to share on the subject.

Allison stared at Rhonda. "What flowers?"

Instead of answering, Rhonda rose and opened the door to Allison's office. The room, though smaller, was almost a carbon copy of her father's, except that she had a computer. And her blinds were opened to admit a view of the ocean, something she had insisted on. The only thing she had insisted on.

"Those flowers." With a flourish Rhonda gestured to a large arrangement of forget-me-nots that stood in the center of Allison's desk. Sitting in a straw basket, the flowers looked completely out of place amid the sleek lines of the office. Everything within the room was utilitarian. The flowers were soft, feminine, delicate. They stirred feelings within her, emotions that made her yearn. She had no idea for what.

She looked at Rhonda. There had to be some sort of mistake. "They're for me?"

Rhonda nodded. "Your name's on them."

"But who—?" No one sent her flowers. Ever. She never had that type of a relationship with anyone. Even the men she had gone out with on the random occasions that she socialized weren't the type to send flowers. They were more cerebral, practical.

Flowers weren't practical. They died, leaving behind only a fragrant memory. A memory that lingered on.

Allison crossed to the desk slowly and slid her finger along a petal. It was soft, silky. Again the longing came, a restlessness that filled her as it confused her.

"Why don't you open the card?" Rhonda prodded. "I already did."

Allison slanted her a glance. "Yes, I know."

It was a handwritten note, one that she was certain came from Angelo rather than from a florist taking an order over the phone. The scrawl was large, lazy. It made her think of him. Even if Rhonda hadn't told her, Allison wouldn't have had to look at the signature to know that the flowers had come from him.

"Looking forward to working with you. Angelo," read the note.

She looked down at the flowers. For a moment she allowed herself to savor the sight and the scent. The office could do with a bit more color like this, she thought. Then she realized that Rhonda was still watching her, her eyes drinking all this in as if it were some classic romance on late night television. Allison dropped the card carelessly onto her desk. "When did these get here?"

Rhonda picked up the card and returned it to its envelope, then propped it against the basket. "About five minutes ago." She sighed. "He works fast."

Yes. Allison set her jaw. She knew the type. "Too fast."

Rhonda gave her a knowing look. "I'd say you could use some of that."

They had a very odd relationship, she and Rhonda. It wasn't the typical boss and secretary variety. Rhonda was as close to a friend as Allison allowed herself to have. Perhaps they had closed ranks because they were two women in a world predominately populated by men. Or perhaps, Allison thought, in her own off-the-wall way, Rhonda had sensed that Allison needed someone to talk to once in a while, if only about things that didn't matter.

Rhonda fussed with the arrangement. "You need a man in your life."

Allison took off her jacket and hung it on the back of her chair. "I have lots of men in my life."

"I don't mean construction workers, although they've got their merits." Rhonda's eyes fairly sparkled. "I mean a guy who'll send you flowers." She tapped the envelope. "Like this one."

Allison glared at the flowers. "He's a construction worker, too." And probably thinks he's the hottest thing in jeans.

Rhonda's grin grew wider still as her imagination took off. "Even better."

Allison sat down and pulled her chair up against the desk. She deliberately moved the basket of flowers to the far side. "Rhonda, don't you have a program to run?"

The other woman nodded. "But I'd rather run your life for a few minutes."

Allison was already pulling a file open on her computer. "Just get me that phone number."

Rhonda toyed with a flower. "Angelo's, right?"

She knew that tone. Rhonda was playing matchmaker. "I have something to discuss with Mr. Marino."

Rhonda crossed to the door. Allison knew she wouldn't let up. After all, the man had sent flowers. "Open dialogue is always good."

Allison looked at her. There was a slight, warning flutter in her stomach. Suddenly she didn't want to talk to Angelo. Calling him now would only seem like an excuse to talk to him. And she didn't want to give out any signals that he might misunderstand. "On second thought get me his partner, Shad McClellan, on the line."

Rhonda paused in the doorway. "What does he look like?"

Allison went back to work, keying in a code that brought up a screen she needed. "It doesn't matter what he looks like. McClellan's married."

She had just secured the data she wanted when the phone buzzed on her desk. Allison hit the speaker button. "Yes?"

"I've got Angelo Marino on the line," Rhonda told her cheerfully.

Allison swore under her breath. She picked the receiver up. "Rhonda, I thought I told you I wanted to talk to McClellan."

"He's busy."

Rhonda's innocent tone didn't fool Allison for a second. She'd made no attempt to get McClellan on the line. "I'll bet."

Rhonda knew her boss well enough to guess what Allison was thinking. "You can't fire me, Sonny. I'm a union member."

"Don't tempt me." Allison closed her eyes, gathering strength. "Okay, put him on." She heard Rhonda's soft chuckle in the background.

Chapter Four

They were on their way out of the mall when Angelo suddenly stopped in front of a florist's stand located near the rear exit. "You've got her card, don't you?"

Shad pulled it out of his pocket and held it up. "This?"

Angelo plucked the card out of his brother's fingers. "Thanks."

Shad shoved his hands into his pockets, resigned to waiting while Angelo set wheels in motion that might very well affect the rest of his life. As far as Shad was concerned, the woman was affecting him already. Angelo ordering flowers. Shad smiled to himself. He was going to have an earful for Dottie and J.T. tonight. He glanced at his watch. If they ever got out of the mall.

"And deliver those right away," Angelo said, passing an extra ten dollars to the thin-faced young man behind the small counter.

The bill disappeared into the man's pocket with lightning speed. "You bet!"

"Can we go now?" Shad asked Angelo.

"Sure."

Shad pushed open the glass door leading out of the mall. Angelo was right behind him, a little more bounce to his step than normal.

"So," Angelo began, shoving his wallet into his back pocket, "what did you think of her?"

Shad chose his words carefully. There were feelings to consider. "She looks very competent." They walked through the parking lot in the general direction of Shad's car.

The assessment wasn't exactly what Angelo had expected to hear. He waited as Shad hit the button unlocking the passenger door. "A computer looks competent." Sitting down, he tugged the seat belt into place.

"That's my point exactly."

Angelo raised his voice as Shad turned on the engine and music filled the small car. "I think I'm missing it."

Shad had always been good with words. Right now he knew he was falling short. This mattered. "Angie, she's very pretty. No, she's a knockout." He looked behind him to make sure the road was clear, then pulled out. "But I always pictured you with someone with warmth. Someone with, you know, like a pulse."

Angelo could see some validity in Shad's observation. "She's reserved."

"She's a rock." Shad saw the flash of annoyance cross Angelo's dark brow. He held up a hand, then replaced it on the wheel as he took a corner to get out of the lot. "Hey, look big brother, I just don't want to see you get hurt, that's all."

They stopped at a light, and Shad turned toward the man he had known and loved for the better part of his life. They shared no blood, but they shared a lifetime of memories. Angelo was always the one who came through for everyone. "There's a lot of love inside there." Shad tapped a finger in the center of Angelo's solid chest. "And I don't want Ms. Conrad-and-Son to walk across it in her three-inch heels, that's all." The light changed and Shad threaded his way up toward the incline that would lead him onto the freeway.

"I can take care of myself."

"True. On the construction site," Shad pointed out. "You can straw-boss and strike fear into men's hearts with the best of them." He slanted a look at Angelo before he took the curve that fed into the freeway. "But let's face it, around someone like that woman, you're a bowl of mush."

It was a case of mistaking "easygoing" for "pushover." Angelo was used to people thinking that. He never saw the need to flex his muscles. When the time came, he always got his way. "That's *Mr.* Mush to you."

Shad laughed, and Angelo joined in. What would be, Shad remembered Salvator Marino always saying, would be. Shad leaned back in the driver's seat as he settled into a lane. "You're really hooked on this woman I take it."

The grin was wide and contented. Anticipation ripened the corners of Angelo's sensual mouth. "Yeah."

"Why?" Why this one and not all the others who had looked at Angelo with longing in their young eyes ever since Shad could remember.

Angelo shrugged. He hadn't thought it all out himself, really. But when he saw Allison this morning, when he touched her, something had just clicked. It was enough. He knew she was the one. "Why's the sky blue, Daddy?"

Shad switched lanes, moving to the left and increasing his speed. "Is that your philosophical way of saying you don't know?"

Angelo answered with a question of his own. They had had a similar conversation three years ago. Only then their positions had been reversed. "Why'd you dig in and decide to wait out J.T.?"

"Because she was sexy and attractive." He thought of the way she had been last night after the children finally fell asleep and they were alone. Soft, alluring. The need that rippled through him almost made him groan. It was wonderful to feel this way about your wife. But then he had known he would from the start. "She still is."

"So are a lot of other women."

"And she needed me." J.T. hadn't known it at the time, but she did.

"So does Allison."

The sign announcing their exit came up and Shad switched lanes again. "Yeah, I noticed." The woman had practically cut Angelo off dead, for God's sake.

Angelo had expected Shad, of all people, to understand. "It isn't anything she said. It's just something I feel." He had seen it in her eyes, sensed it in her manner. Angelo looked at his brother and searched his face for awareness. "You know what I mean?"

Shad thought back to his own rocky start with J.T. She'd wanted no part of him, either, and had literally tried to shut the door in his face. He had stuck his foot in. That had been the beginning. "Yeah, I know what you mean." Easing off the freeway, he took a corner. "So the flowers were for her?"

"And for Dottie." Angelo had figured that while he was at it, why not?

Shad didn't understand. "You sent Dottie flowers?"

Angelo realized that Shad had forgotten their conversation on the way over. "A guy's sister only has her first baby once."

Shad shook his head. Angelo had a heart bigger than Anaheim Stadium. He worried again about it being trampled. "You're about seven months premature." But he knew Dottie would be tickled silly.

Angelo rolled down the window and let the wind hit his face. Usually that was enough to relax him. This time it wasn't. Adrenaline seemed to be coursing through his body. "I like being the first one."

Angelo, who loved sleeping in. Angelo, who was always so laid-back. "Is this something new?"

"Yeah." The feel of having Allison's body tangled with his suddenly came back to him. He felt his body hum. "I'm turning over a new leaf."

The Houghton Building loomed ahead of them. It was a three-story building with manicured lawns and Italian stone pine trees flanking either side of the front walk. They had offices on the ground floor. Shad pulled up into the parking lot and found a shady spot. "Just as long as you don't start an avalanche."

"That's with snow, Shad, not leaves."

"I'm a native Southern Californian. What do I know about snow?" He pulled up the hand brake. "Want to grab a bite to eat before getting back?"

Normally he'd say yes. But this wasn't a normal time for Angelo. "Naw, I've got some details to clear up if we're going to give our full attention to the mall for the next few months." He unfolded his body and got out of the car. There were a lot more comfortable modes of transportation, but Shad loved the car, so Angelo voiced no complaints about the accommodations.

Shad looked at him over the hood of the Jaguar and raised a brow knowingly. "The mall?"

Angelo laughed. He rocked back on the balls of his feet as anticipation danced through him again. God, it felt good to be alive. "Nobody ever said you can't mix business with pleasure."

"At least not in my hearing." Shad closed his door and pressed the security lock, then fell into step beside Angelo. They walked into the building together. The first door to the left was theirs. "Dottie'll appreciate the flowers, Angelo. Nice touch."

Angelo thought of the woman who had walked out of Walters's office, shoulders straight like a retreating soldier. "I hope our co-contractor has the same reaction."

"Phone, Mr. Marino," Shirley announced just as he and Shad walked past her desk. With an encouraging smile the woman held up the receiver.

"Speak of the devil?" Shad guessed, looking quizzically at Angelo

"That's no way to refer to your future sister-in-law," Angelo told him. It was too soon for her to call, wasn't it? He felt just the slightest jangle of nerves. He took it as an indication that he had assessed his reactions correctly. He had never been nervous about a woman before.

Angelo saw the secretary he and Shad shared look at him with renewed interest. New gossip for the office. But he didn't care who knew it.

"Thanks, Shirley. I'll take it in my office."

Angelo closed the door behind him. Crossing to his desk quickly, he made himself comfortable in the oversize office chair before he placed his hand on the receiver. He conjured up a mental image of Allison in his mind, the way she had looked, staring down at him after the dog yanked them together, surprise highlighting her features, the sun framing her head, her body intimately pressing against his.

Changing his mind, he left the receiver alone and pressed down the speakerphone instead. He wanted her voice to fill the room and surround him. "Marino."

"Why did you send me flowers?" Allison demanded.

Ah, the voice of love. She just didn't know it yet. "It seemed like the thing to do." He grinned. "This is Allison, right?"

It took her a second to assimilate the name. Everyone always called her Sonny. Trust him to be different. "Why, how many flowers did you ship out today?"

He sat up and straightened a photograph of Dottie and her crew on his desk. He'd have to get a new one once the baby came. "I sent my sister a bouquet. I just found out she's expecting her first baby."

Because Allison was so attuned to competing in a man's world she had honed all the necessary skills at her disposal to perfection. A quick wit had always been her greatest asset, right after determination and tenacity. It was devastating to discover that her mind had completely deserted her at a time when she needed it most.

"You sent your sister flowers?" The question sounded painfully dumb to her ears, yet his innocent statement had caught her completely off guard. It didn't jibe with her impression of him. Was that his intent, to throw her off?

"Sure." He heard the disbelief in her voice and wondered why she sounded so distrustful. "Why not?"

No one was as nice as he was pretending to be. "Do you get them wholesale?"

He decided to match her flippancy for the moment. "I pick them in my backyard. Yours were forget-me-nots." Tea roses had gone to Dottie. Yellow ones. They were her favorite.

She looked at them. It was hard to be mad at a basket of flowers. But she tried. "Oh, I'm not about to forget you."

It sounded like a threat, but he decided to ignore that aspect. "I hope not."

She hadn't meant to feed his ego. Flustered and annoyed at him for making her feel that way, she suddenly remembered her father's demand. "This isn't a social call, Mr Marino."

He leaned back in his chair. He hadn't thought this was going to be a piece of cake. But he was up to the challenge. "No, I suspect not. You sound as if you'd rather have me drawn and quartered than be social."

She didn't like to be thought of as rude, even by him. She disliked rude people. It was just that he seemed to bring out the worst in her. She wasn't about to play the simpering colleen to his macho construction worker. "I didn't mean to be ill-tempered. The flowers are very pretty—"

"Not nearly as pretty as you," Angelo said quickly. "But I thought they got my message across a lot better than roses."

If she had any sense, she'd push the flowers into the wastepaper basket. But the flowers stayed where they were. "And what message is that?"

"I'd like to get to know you, Allison." A lot better, he added silently.

She stiffened, even though he wasn't there to see it. "We'll be working together for the next four months." And she suddenly wished they wouldn't be. She didn't like being unsettled. And he made her feel that way.

That wasn't good enough and they both knew it, although he would take what he could get at the moment. "People work alongside each other for years and never get to know anything about the other person."

She thought of her father. She had been his daughter for twenty-nine years, and he didn't even know her favorite color, or what made her smile. But that was her father, not a big, overgrown clumsy oaf who thought she'd fall into his arms if he tossed flowers at her. "What's your point, Marino?"

Angelo noticed that the "Mister" had been dropped from in front of his name. He liked her this way, feisty instead of frosty. Where there was a fire he knew he could eventually warm himself. And fully intended to. "I don't plan on that happening between us."

Plans? He was making plans? Without thinking Allison crumpled the paper under her hand. "Marino, there isn't going to be an 'us.'"

Beneath the snap he thought he detected a note of fear. What was she afraid of? "That's for time to decide."

The gall of the man. Just who did he think he was? God's gift to women? "No, that's for *me* to decide. I call the shots in my life."

She came across as one tough lady. No one was that tough unless they were trying too hard to protect a vulnerable side. He leaned back and put his feet up on the desk. "Sometimes Fate steps in."

"My dog? What does my dog have to do with it?" Next he'd be claiming to be able to communicate with animals.

He could visualize her in her office, the full lips drawn into a frown, the small line that appeared between her brows when she was annoyed. "Specifically he introduced us, but I was thinking of something a little more mystical than a Great Dane."

She wasn't going to waste any more time getting angry. The only way to handle this was to change the subject. "I'd like to get down to business Marino."

"So would I." All sorts of business, he thought. Some productive, some personal.

She sighed, drumming her fingers on the desk. She'd worked with blockheads before. She could do it again. Their reputation was at stake. "I'd like a list of buildings you've worked on."

He found he enjoyed teasing her. She needed to lighten up before she exploded. He was just the man to do it. "If it's character references you want..." He began to doodle on the blotter. It was covered with calculations for rough estimates alongside some rather artistic cartoon figures.

She fought the urge to scream into the receiver. If there was one professional bone in this man's body, she was going to find it, even if she had to take apart all the rest piece by piece. "What I want is what I said—a list of your buildings. My father is interested in the quality of your work. Our name is going to be linked with yours—"

"Yes."

She knew he meant something entirely different than she did. In a voice that stopped quarreling construction workers in their tracks and restored order, she said, "Don't play games with me, Marino. I don't play games."

And that's your trouble. "Maybe you should start."

She wished she had him here alone for just five minutes. "Damn it, Marino, you're deliberately trying to unnerve me. If you were standing in front of me right now, you'd be wearing your forget-me-nots as well as the imprint of my shoe strategically planted. And I promise you it wouldn't be landing on your all-too-big ego."

Laughter met her words, and she bit back a few choicer, stronger words. Swearing probably wouldn't get her any place, anyway. "The list, Marino, by tomorrow morning." She slammed down the phone so hard that it bounced off the cradle.

"She loves me." Angelo grinned as he pressed down the speakerphone connection again, cutting short the whine of the dial tone.

Shad had been drawn by the sound of the conversation and had opened the door. They had always made a habit of butting into each other's life. He saw no reason to stop now. It sounded as if Angelo needed help. The medical kind.

"Loves you?" he echoed. "You never had your head X-rayed after Daniels accidentally beaned you, did you?"

Angelo took no offense at Shad's words. "It's not my head, Shad. It's my heart."

Shad crossed to his desk and sat on the corner of it, looking down at his brother. "It's your hearing if you think that woman even remotely likes you. She sounded as if she'd take great pleasure in seeing you neutered."

The look in Angelo's eyes turned serious. "People say a lot of things when they're scared."

"Scared? Of what?" Shad hadn't changed his initial assessment of Allison Conrad. She looked like a lady who could spit bullets. Which was fine. He just didn't want her doing it in Angelo's direction.

Angelo laced his fingers behind his head. "Of me."

Shad shook his head. "Well, you are pretty repulsive, but—"

Angelo decided not to continue the thread of Shad's banter. Instead he softened his voice. "I think she's afraid of getting close to a guy."

"All this in one meeting?" It seemed like an awful lot of insight to him. Analyzing was Dottie's department, not Angelo's.

Angelo held up two fingers. "Two. Don't forget I ran into her this morning." Swinging his feet from the desk, he pushed back his chair and rose. "And even once is enough if it's the right one."

Shad rose, as well. "Now you sound just like Ma."

Angelo shrugged good-naturedly. "The woman has to be right once in a while."

Shad thought of the look on Allison's face as she left the office. And the sound of her voice just now. "You'll pardon me if I don't rent a tuxedo yet."

"You've got time."

Shad headed out the door. "Thanks."

"Four months," Angelo called after him.

Shad just shook his head and kept walking.

Allison told herself that the reason she dressed so carefully the following Monday morning was because she wanted to get the right message across to that Neanderthal she was forced to cooperate with. And the message was: competent business woman, expert engineer. More specifically, a woman who would break both his kneecaps if he came within ten feet of her with anything more intimate than a blueprint. It was hard to get all that into a light gray pair of slacks with a matching oversize jacket.

She surveyed herself in the full-length mirror in her room as she chewed her lower lip. Maybe the dusty rose cowl neck blouse was too bright, too cheerful. Not authoritative enough. She glanced at her watch. There wasn't enough time to change, not if she didn't want to be late. She frowned.

He'd like that—her being late. Well, she wasn't going to be, even if she had picked the wrong blouse.

She pushed the sleeves of her jacket up impatiently. She wished she could take her dog with her.

Allison ran a hand over her face and took in two deep, cleansing breaths. What the hell was the matter with her? She was acting as if this was a prom date instead of a preliminary meeting to settle any outstanding questions about their work schedule. She should just wear jeans and a work shirt the way she usually did on a construction site.

In the background she heard the sound of the Lincoln. Jeremy, the three-hundred-pound former wrestler who was her father's chauffeur and doubled as a bodyguard, was driving Miles to the office. She let out a sigh of relief. At least he wasn't going to give her any last-minute instructions as if she were some sort of wet-behind-the-ears grunt.

In the past five years she had taken more and more upon herself. She could point to her handiwork in a dozen different structures. The Topaz Hotel in Palm Springs was hers. The architect's name was on the design, but it was her hand that had brought it to life, her ingenuity that had found a way to make it all work, striking fanciful things that had no way of existing except in the mind of an artist, yet retaining the beauty of it. She had brought a two-dimensional drawing to life in the real world. Everyone had lavished praise on her for a job more than well-done when she completed the hotel. James Topaz, a third-generation billionaire, had been extremely attentive, as well as grateful. Only her father had found fault in her work.

But he was good at that.

The reflection in the mirror appeared nervous, unsettled, as if waiting for a storm to break. She pressed her lips together. She had easily turned down James Topaz when his display of gratitude included a weekend away in Paris as his "guest." Why were her palms damp and itchy now? She looked down and realized she was rubbing her thumb against her forefinger.

She damned the husky male voice that had played through her head all through the night, keeping her awake. When this extension was done, she was going to have Angelo Marino's head on a platter.

"Don't look now, but I think she's loaded for bear." Shad nudged Angelo as he saw Allison approaching them, crossing the parking lot.

Angelo turned. His pulse quickened just a shade as he watched her walking toward them. Toward him. There was an unconscious sway to her hips. She'd be angry if she knew the kind of signals she was sending out. Angelo felt a very primitive urge thrum through him, an urge akin to the one that had made demands on him during that first encounter on the grass. Friday. When his life was forever changed.

They had chosen to meet outside the mall on the grounds that would eventually become the Emerald Plaza. Angelo and Shad had set up a table. Blueprints were spread across it. Not a single leaf stirred. Even the winds were at her command, Angelo thought.

His eyes never left Allison's form as she drew closer across the lot. "Maybe I can learn to growl like a bear," he finally replied.

Shad shook his head. "I don't think it's your voice she's interested in." He glanced at Angelo. "I think the lady wants to skin you."

She was aware that he had watched her every step, and it had served to make her incredibly self-conscious. Another strike against him. No one else had ever managed to do that to her except for her father. She prided herself on always appearing self-possessed. Angelo was ruining that.

Dropping her briefcase next to the table, she pulled the basket of flowers he had sent out of the shopping bag she was carrying and thrust it at him. "I think we'll be better off if you take these back."

Because he had no choice he took them from her. "I've never gotten flowers from a lady before."

He had her teeth on edge and they hadn't been together two minutes yet. "You're not *getting* them. I'm *returning* them."

Angelo didn't seem to hear. He set the flowers on the table next to the blueprints. "I don't need forget-me-nots to remember you."

She looked at Shad for help. "Is he always this dense?" she asked in exasperation.

Shad grinned and crossed his arms. There was no arguing that the lady cut a nice figure. He had to admire Angelo's taste, if not his common sense. "He had the thickest head in the neighborhood."

Allison addressed her words to Shad. She was banking on the fact that since the company was a success, at least one of the men had to be reasonably intelligent. That meant it had to be Shad. "I would like this arrangement to work."

Angelo moved behind Shad in order to get into her line of vision. He presented her with the list she had asked for the other day. "No more than I."

Shad saw a dangerous flare enter Allison's eyes as she glanced at the list, then shoved it into her pocket. "He means 'we,'" Shad corrected.

Allison tried again. "Conrad and Son has a reputation to maintain."

"It won't be compromised," Angelo promised, raising one hand in a pledge. "Unless you want it to," he added under his breath.

She turned from Shad and raised her eyes to Angelo's. "Marino, I'd like you to keep one thing in mind."

"What?"

"They've done away with the death penalty in this state. Even for murder," she added significantly.

She turned toward Shad, her voice completely business-like. "Now, then, I've brought along a list of points I'd like to go over with you." Shad pulled out one of the three folding chairs that surrounded the table. She sat down, satisfied that Angelo had gotten the message once and for all.

Shad could guess that by the expression on her face. He figured her assumption came from the fact that she didn't know Angelo very well.

But she would. Shad made a mental note to mark his calendar for four months hence. Tuxedo fittings were always hard to work in at the last minute.

Chapter Five

Allison arrived early on the site each day, usually before any of her crew showed up. She had always preferred hands-on work to the kind that could be done from behind a desk. She liked seeing the structure take shape. Each problem was a challenge, each challenge a triumph in disguise.

It made the burden she carried with her a little easier to bear.

She kept on top of everything with an eagle eye for problems. The schedule was uppermost in her mind. They had to stay ahead. Each missed deadline had its own hefty penalty. Conrad and Son had never had to pay a single penalty. She intended to see that the record remained unchanged.

Ground-breaking proceeded without a hitch. Keeping four crews working longer hours and Saturdays, the complete foundation for the extension was laid within two weeks. Then framing started. She was pleased that the other half of the extension wasn't even a half beat behind. Maybe Marino wasn't as bad as she thought. At least professionally.

Conrad and Son and Marino and McClellan had divided the work as equitably as possible. Her company was to handle the west wing, Marino and McClellan were to do the east. Trouble, she assumed, would arise when it came to doing the north section. That they were splitting down the middle. It would either be a triumph of cooperation and teamwork, or a Tower of Babel. She was hoping for a triumph. She was anticipating Babel.

Allison pushed a pencil impatiently into her hair right behind her ear. She was spending too much time thinking about what was going on at the other construction site. Too much time thinking about that man. Too much time anticipating trouble where there might not be any.

Ha.

Trouble had a name and it was Angelo Marino. Just because things had been going well so far didn't lull her into a false feeling of complacency. She knew better She didn't know how; she just did. It was like waiting for a bomb to drop. She knew it was going to; she just didn't know where or when. But it was going to—she'd bet her life on it.

She had already seen the warning signs. Initially she had naively assumed that since he was a professional and since the construction work was being conducted behind the plywood fences that separated the stores of the existing mall from its extension, she was relatively safe. Angelo would stay on his side and she on hers.

Wrong.

Allison discovered that he could find a dozen excuses a day to come over to her side and seek her out to talk to. She never knew where he'd turn up next, and it made her jumpy. She figured it was because he got on her nerves, *not* that he got under her skin.

"Sonny, did you hear anything I said?"

She looked up into the face of her assistant, a tall, thin man whose sleepy-eyed demeanor belied a sharp mind. She had only heard half of what he'd said. Damn, now Marino was interfering with her thinking process. It *had* to stop.

"Of course I heard you." She frowned as she quickly scanned the clipboard Joseph had handed her to orient herself. On it were sheets pertaining to the plumbing installation. "Tell Browne his projection is unacceptable. I need the pipes to be installed on that block of stores by next Friday, not the week after."

Joseph ran his hand through his wheat-colored hair. It was as close as he usually came to combing it. "I'll tell him, but I don't think—"

No, Joseph would be too easygoing. She knew that. What was she thinking of? "Never mind. I'll do it." There was no snap of impatience in her words, the way there would have been if her father was saying the very same thing to her. She wasn't annoyed; she was just relieving Joseph of another burden. And taking it onto her shoulders.

She took out the portable phone she carried with her on the job and punched out the numbers she wanted. She kept a complete list of phone numbers in her head and rarely had to refer to a book to find the one she needed. As soon as a job was over, the numbers would vanish from her memory.

"Edgar Browne, please," she said in answer to the secretary's inquiry on the other end. "Tell him Conrad and Son is calling."

That was the way Angelo found her, one hand holding a clipboard, the other a telephone. He had arrived on the site at six, spending the morning hours going over various calculations that needed altering. By eleven he had decided he needed a break and headed toward the west wing.

The cavernous area was a deafening mixture of noise, dust, men and girders. He had to weave his way carefully in some areas to avoid tripping over coils of wire or rope. Other parts were completely empty, except for the chalky dust that was everywhere. It was hard to believe that this mess would eventually rise up into a beautiful, tidy structure where people would come to spend their money or their time. But it did. Every time.

He enjoyed working with his hands and his mind. Having Allison close by added to his pleasure. In the three weeks that had passed he hadn't changed his mind. His first impression had been on the money.

This was the one. There was no doubt in his mind.

It didn't hurt that she was in the business and understood the same language he did. It was a plus. What was a minus was her total absorption in it, as if anything that existed outside of work was meaningless. He was just going to have to nudge her along until she realized that there was a whole life waiting for her to sample.

Allison finished signing her name to an order form that one of the other assistants brought to her. She had just shoved her pencil behind her ear when she heard a voice come on the line. She waved at an approaching construction worker, indicating that he should wait a minute.

"Yes, Ed, Sonny here. He's fine, thanks," she said in answer to Browne's inquiry after her father's health.

If Miles Conrad was on his deathbed, he wouldn't tolerate her saying anything else except that he was fine. His private life had absolutely no place in his business life. It was something he had drummed into her head, as well.

"What's not fine is your work projection. Yes, I know you're busy, but so are we." Her eyes narrowed as she pressed her lips together. She had no patience with slow and steady when one could finish a job quickly. "Look, Ed, it took God six days to create the world. If you can't bring plumbing to a tiny section of a mall in two weeks, I'm afraid I'll have to get someone else to—oh, you can." The corners of her mouth softened as satisfaction filled it out.

Watching, Angelo had the overwhelming urge to brush a kiss to each corner. And then to take her into his arms and finish the job properly. He was looking forward to that, and it would be soon, he promised himself. He couldn't wait much longer.

"I see. Well, that's fine, Ed. I'll see you on the site tomorrow." She pressed a button on the phone, cutting the connection. She was very pleased with herself as she returned the phone to its case. One problem down, five hundred to go.

Angelo moved out of the way as two workers passed him, dragging a sawhorse between them. He crossed the short distance to Allison. "You look very satisfied."

"I am." She gave the clipboard back to Joseph and turned around. Then her eyes narrowed again. "You."

It wasn't exactly a warm reception, but it didn't deter him. Angelo shrugged. "It's a small site."

Why did he insist on popping up all the time? "Not by my measurements."

He grinned. "Maybe we should go over your measurements together sometime."

Allison turned away and walked to the blueprints spread out on the table. He never missed a step. She turned, hands on hips. "Marino, things would go a lot smoother if you kept to your side."

Angelo made sure work was progressing smoothly before he ventured over to her side. Although he had a campaign to wage, he never lost sight of the work he had to do, or the people who relied on him.

"I like to keep tabs on the overall picture. For that I need to see how your side is going." Even amid all this dust that was constantly being kicked up, he could smell her. She used something herbal in her hair. A softer, lighter fragrance clung to her shirt. He wondered if it clung to her skin, as well. It was something to find out.

She raised her chin defensively. She didn't like someone keeping tabs on her. For any reason. It made her feel trapped. "My side's going fine. Don't your people need you for something?"

Angelo made no move to go. "Not at the moment." He saw the look in her eyes. She obviously thought he wasn't holding up his end. "I trust my people, Allison. That's why I hired them. They do good work. I don't need to look over their shoulder every minute." Angelo indicated the phone that hung off her belt. "You were pretty tough a minute ago."

Her fingers spread over the telephone. It made Angelo think of a gunfighter reaching for his holster. "A woman in a man's world has to be."

Yes, he could see that. He could see her being tough, not relying on or taking advantage of the fact that she was beautiful enough to melt a man's kneecaps. She played it straight and matched them at their own game. He admired her for it, but there was such a thing as going too far. "Don't you lose sight of you?"

She had no time to be analyzed, especially by someone who didn't seem to think he had to do more than show up at a site to justify his existence. "I have a very clear picture of me, Marino." She spread her hands wide, indicating the area around her. "This *is* me."

She might believe that, but he didn't. There was something softer, more delicate, almost vulnerable beneath the efficient woman who barked orders to a squadron of men she surrounded herself with. She wasn't just "Son" of Conrad and Son. She was something more. Some*one* more.

She didn't like the way he was looking at her, as if he saw something she was unsure of, something she didn't want to know about. "Did you come over for a specific reason, or just to gawk at me?"

The angrier she got, the more he seemed to enjoy himself. She was fighting it, but she'd come around. Soon, if he didn't miss his guess. "Yes, not that gawking at you isn't a pleasure, but there is a specific reason."

She held her hand up, stopping him, afraid of what he might have to say. There were too many people around to hear. She looked toward Joseph.

The man knew when to make an exit. Joseph tucked the clipboard under his arm. "I'm going on break for a few minutes, Sonny." As he backed away, he exchanged grins with the man on Allison's other side.

Allison had forgotten there was someone still waiting. She turned to him. "And you?"

He looked a little intimidated. "I just wanted to tell you that the tiles for the ground-floor courtyard finally arrived."

"Fine," she snapped, then dragged her hand across her bangs. She flashed the man an apologetic look. "I'm sorry, Jake. It's been a long morning." She slanted Angelo a look. *And it's about to get longer.*

"No problem." Jake laughed, but he retreated from the area quickly.

Allison closed her eyes. When she opened them, Angelo was still standing there in front of her. Somehow she knew he would be, even though she had hoped he'd take a blatant hint. "I really wish you'd stay on your own side. You're undermining my authority with the men, hanging around like this."

Not to mention that you're playing havoc with my thinking process.

Why was that?

Another girder was being lifted into place and the riveting was almost deafening. Angelo took her arm and ushered her to another, slightly more private area. "Why should I stay away? Are you afraid they won't think of you as the iron maiden?"

She pulled her arm away. She didn't want him touching her It did things to her that she didn't want done. "I don't want them to think they're privy to some soap opera unfolding in front of them.

"A person can get hooked on soap operas."

"I wouldn't know. I don't watch television." He was probably a couch potato when he got home at night. No, she amended, not with that body. You didn't get hard muscles from lying around eating chips and drinking beer. "I don't have the time."

He wondered what she did with herself when she wasn't being an engineer. There had to be something. "What do you have the time for?"

He was wasting her time. She looked beyond his head and watched the girder rise. There was something lyrical about a structure coming together. Power and grace. A perfect marriage. What more could she ask for than to be a part of that? "My work."

He already knew that. "And?"

Her eyes shifted back to Angelo. What did he want from her? "There is no 'and.'"

Did she think she began and ended on a site? "I saw you jogging that first day."

She shrugged. "That's to clear my head. I need regular exercise."

He hooked his thumbs in his jeans and studied her face. There was a lot going on behind her eyes that he didn't fully understand yet. "What do you do, Allison?"

What was that supposed to mean? "I'm a contractor in case you haven't noticed."

He shook his head. The woman was stubborn. "I mean for fun."

Was the man deaf? Or maybe he was too thick to understand. "I jog."

"We seem to be into reruns here. I meant besides that."

She thought for a moment. She liked to take long, hot showers, with the steam curling up around her, misting the mirrors and enveloping her in a feeling of well-being. But that was far too personal a thing to tell him. God only knows what he'd make of it. "I read."

He refused to give up. There had to be a crack in there somewhere. When he found it, he was going through. "Do you do anything that involves more than one person?"

She looked at him pointedly. Marino was probably referring to "indoor sports." Neanderthals were like that. One-track minds. It was a track, if she were being honest with herself—and *only* with herself—that she kept sliding toward ever since this project started. But that was her problem and he didn't need to know. "No."

"Would you like to try a new experience?"

She was trying very hard to dislike him. It wasn't as easy as it looked. There was something about him that pulled at her. Perhaps it could be chalked up to some sort of basic animal attraction. He was very attractive, if not handsome. Manly was a better word. But whatever the appropriate description, the response would be the same. She wanted no part of anything he had to offer her.

She placed a hand in the center of his chest, indicating she wanted him out of the way. But he didn't budge. Blowing out a breath between her teeth, she walked around him. "What I would like to try, Marino—" she glared at him over her shoulder "—is getting this job done on time and I can't do that if you're standing in my way."

He raised his hands in a sign of peace. "Okay, I'll go."

She looked toward the sky, the picture of relief. "There is a God."

Then came the rest. "On one condition."

She shut her eyes, searching for strength. She kept them shut as she asked, "Which is?"

Angelo moved so that he was in front of her again. "You'll have coffee with me."

Although work hadn't stopped, she was certain they were the center of everyone's attention. She had to get rid of this man. "I don't—"

Angelo wouldn't let her finish. "And don't tell me you don't drink coffee, I've seen you put it away by the gallon.

It's a wonder they don't have to pry you off the roof at night."

She didn't like her habits analyzed. What she did was her business. "Is that how you get your kicks, spying on women?"

The fire in her eyes just made her that much sexier. He found it difficult keeping his hands at his sides when all he wanted to do was hold her. "Not women. A woman. Singular. You."

Why was there a warm shiver dancing through her when he said that? She had no time for his advances, even if they were genuine, which she knew they weren't. His type never was. "If I'm supposed to be flattered—"

"No, just informed."

Allison passed her hands over her face, then laced them in front of her. She surrendered. But only so far. "If I have coffee with you, will you go away?"

He had come to ask her out for coffee to begin with. "You drive a hard bargain, but okay."

She waited for him to leave. He didn't. "Now?"

"That was the idea." He glanced at his watch. "Eleven-fifteen seems like a good time to take a break." An easy smile curved his lips. "Unless, of course, you want an early lunch." She hardly ever stopped for lunch. He'd seen her taking stock of the work, a half-eaten sandwich forgotten in her hand.

If she didn't stop him, he'd be on another roll. She held up her hand like a traffic policeman, holding back oncoming cars. "Coffee, just coffee."

"If you have a sandwich with me, that doesn't mean we're engaged."

She looked at him oddly. "Has anyone ever told you that you're a really strange person?"

"Most of my family," he said lightly. "But I don't pay attention to them." Turning, he took her arm as he began to walk toward the curtained section in front of him. The mall lay beyond.

She tried to pull away, but he wouldn't let her. "I can walk under my own power, Marino."

"That's one of the things I find charming about you," he returned without missing a beat. As they passed a scaffold, he glanced up out of habit. Uttering a curse, he shoved her out of the way, pushing Allison against a plywood wall with the momentum from his own body.

"Hey!" With the air knocked out of her Allison still managed to wedge her hands between them, pushing hard against his chest. It was like pushing against granite. She dusted him with a few choice words that only brought a chuckle from him.

Angelo was acutely aware of every single curve in her body as it fitted against his. Desire flared full bloom through his own. Allison's eyes widened as the very distinct fact registered with her. "Well, here we are again," he murmured. He wanted her. There was no denying that. But he wanted her completely. And forever. That was going to take patience. He'd always had it before. He searched for it now.

She concentrated on shutting out the fact that something was going on inside her. "Something" had very obviously weakened her from the ankles on up. She felt shaky, as if she couldn't get enough air into her lungs. She wasn't shoving him away so much as resting her hands against him, steadying herself. Searching the depths of her soul, she sought out anger. Anger always kept her safe. It had been her shield before.

"What's the big idea, you big, dumb—?"

Reluctantly he released her. "Before you say anything you're going to be very sorry for—" Angelo stepped back and pointed behind him "—I think you should look at that."

"That" was a steel beam that was hanging precariously by one coupling in the exact place where she had been standing only a second ago. By now they were the center of activity as construction workers from all sides came rushing up.

"Oh." She hated being in debt to him, but there was no getting around the fact that he had saved her.

"I'll take that as an apology." He grinned. "Undying gratitude wouldn't hurt, either."

Her knees still felt weak, but for a different reason. She could have been seriously hurt, if not worse if he hadn't been there. "I guess I do owe you an apology."

"I'll settle for you buying the coffee. For now."

"Jeez, Sonny, you okay?" the construction worker closest to her asked, clearly upset.

A chorus of other concerns were voiced all around her.

She shook her head, quieting them. "I'm fine." She looked at the man who had jumped from the scaffold, frightened, and had come running over to her. "Reilly, another one of those accidents and—"

The young man ran his hand nervously through his dark hair. "I know, I know. I swear it won't happen again, Ms. Conrad. Please, I need this job—"

Reilly was having trouble at home, and she knew he was preoccupied. "Nobody's firing you, Reilly. Joseph."

She didn't have to say anything else. Joseph nodded, coming forward. Reilly would be reassigned to something less hazardous. For everyone concerned.

"Okay, show's over," she announced. "Back to work, everyone. We've got deadlines to meet." She turned to Angelo and saw the look of cool admiration on his face. She felt a smile rising in response, although she knew his reaction didn't matter to her one way or another. "Where are we going for coffee? I need to tell Joseph where to find me."

"In case of what?" He brushed back the hair that had fallen into her face. "Can't they get along without you for twenty minutes?"

She jerked her head away. "You make me sound ridiculous."

"No, but there is such a thing as delegating responsibility."

"I do." Grudgingly she walked beside him, wondering if this was such a smart thing to do.

"And trying too hard," he continued.

She stopped walking. "Just because you saved me from having my head split open doesn't mean you get the right to play psychiatrist with what you *think* you see going on in there."

Very firmly he took her hand and linked his fingers with hers. She pulled, but he held on. She gave up. "I promise not to play doctor. Now loosen up and let's have that coffee. I'll have you back before midnight, Cinderella."

She was walking, but she didn't like it. "I don't care for your attitude, Marino."

"That's okay. It'll grow on you."

She glared at him. "I wouldn't place any bets on that if I were you."

He turned to look at her as he held back the tarp. They stepped out into the mall proper. There were people hurrying all around them, making do with a few precious minutes they had allotted for lunch, trying to squeeze in a little shopping. Her resistance didn't bother him. "Would you have guessed when you got up this morning that you'd be having coffee with me by eleven?"

She didn't like the smug look on his face, but she had to be honest. "No."

"See?"

No, she refused to "see." "Marino, I don't mix business with pleasure."

He nodded to the left and she turned. There was a charming French café that served crepes and rich aromatic coffee beneath a blue-and-white-striped canopy, even though it was indoors. "Then it's high time you started seeing the benefits of business and pleasure."

Let him babble all he wanted, she thought resolutely. She was just having coffee with him to make him leave her alone and prevent a scene from happening in front of her people. Besides, she thought, he *had* saved her from a nasty injury. She owed him a cup of coffee.

But that was definitely all she owed him.

Chapter Six

"So how do you feel about being the mother of my children?"

Sweet, thick coffee lodged in Allison's throat in midswallow, refusing to go up or down, choking her. She coughed, trying to pull in air, her eyes watering as she stared incredulously at the man sitting across from her in the restaurant.

Angelo firmly patted Allison on the back. As the coughing subsided, he urged a glass of water on her. Several sips brought her some relief. At least she could talk again. "What—?" Her voice was raspy and she cleared it twice. "What did they put in your coffee?"

He tilted the cup toward him and made a pretense of looking into it. "The usual stuff. It's not the best cappuccino, but for that we'll have to go to my mother's house."

When hell freezes over, she thought.

She straightened up and looked at him in utter disbelief. He was going on as if he hadn't just said the most insane thing she had ever heard. "When you pushed me out of the way before, back on the site, did that beam graze your head by any chance?''

''No,'' he answered, amused. ''Why?''

''Why? Because you just—'' She closed her eyes and then sighed. What was the use? She couldn't talk sensibly to a crazy person. ''I've got to get back.''

She began to move her chair away from the table. Angelo placed his hand over hers. Clear blue eyes looked up into his, waiting. He wondered if she understood that there was nothing in the world he wanted more than to have children with her, to have a small being that was the end result of two people loving each other. Of her loving him. The only thing Angelo wanted more than to have a child look up and call him Daddy was to have Allison love him.

''You didn't answer my question.''

He really *was* crazy. ''I don't think it deserved an answer.''

He grinned at her, somehow inexplicably negating the anger she had felt just a moment ago. Warmth was spreading through her body, warmth that was generated from the touch of his hand. Maybe she was the crazy one.

''Is that another way of saying you'll think about it?'' he asked. A little girl, he decided. They'd have a little girl first. And she'd look just like Allison.

She moved her hand away, dropping it in her lap. It was the only place she thought of that was out of his reach. At least she hoped so. ''That's another way of saying I'll speak to your partner about having you locked up and put away somewhere for your own good—and mine.''

He cocked his head, his eyes skimming along the delicate planes of her face. He wasn't about to give up so easily. ''That's a no, isn't it?''

Nothing less than a two-by-four was going to work here. She was beginning to see that. ''I can't figure out if you're making some sort of joke at my expense or just plain crazy.''

He signaled for the check and the waiter came quickly. Angelo took out a five-dollar bill from his wallet and left it on top of the small blue tray that held the receipt. "Isn't there a third choice?"

"Such as?" she asked suspiciously. Sensibly she knew she shouldn't even be carrying on this conversation. But something kept making her go on. It was as if one word was irresistibly linked to another and she had no choice but to follow the links to the end of the chain no matter what was there. No matter what she feared was there.

"My being head over heels in love with you."

He couldn't be serious. Did he think she was an emptyheaded idiot to fall for a line like that? Or did he somehow know that it was the one secret wish in her heart to be loved by someone. But she knew that wasn't about to happen, even if circumstances were different. And they weren't. She was irrevocably tied to a promise and a way of life.

"That's a bad lyric in a song or juvenile poem, not a sentiment for a man who's past puberty." Her brow rose as she studied him pointedly. "You have passed puberty, haven't you?"

If she meant to insult him, she failed. Angelo had never angered very easily. "Don't pretend you don't like me, Allison."

The only person who had ever called her that was her mother. She frowned as cherished memories fought to break through. She couldn't afford to see Angelo in any other light than the one she cast for him. It would complicate far too many things.

"I don't have to pretend." This time she did get up, pushing her chair away with finality. She used the table between them as a barrier. Her eyes narrowed. "You come within ten feet of me and I'll fix it so that you can hit all the high notes you want."

Undaunted, he smiled. "Then dinner is out?"

Her eyes opened wide. Maybe she was still in shock from the near accident. What did it take to get through to this man? "What dinner?"

Knuckles against the tabletop, he leaned toward her. "With me tonight."

He was wearing some kind of cologne that appealed to her. It tickled her nose, getting into her senses, under her skin. She fought the drugging effects off. "No dinner. Not tonight, not tomorrow, next year or next century."

Nothing seemed to faze him. "I didn't know they made appointment books that far ahead."

She made an angry noise under her breath, swung around on her heel and stormed out, shaking her head. The man was crazy, certifiably crazy. She was going to have to find the time to talk to McClellan and see if something couldn't be done about this. The extension wasn't going to be completed in time, not their part, not hers, if she constantly had to fend off that oversexed suburban cowboy.

And the worst part of it was that he was wearing her down.

The mother of my children.

Allison gritted her teeth as she took a momentary break much later. Angelo's line had been playing and replaying itself in her head all afternoon. She was surprised he hadn't hurried after her when she left the restaurant, grabbed her by her hair and dragged her off to some cave. Surprised and relieved.

The ass, the pompous, pompous ass. The more she thought about the line he had tried to feed her, the more it became one. A stupid, conceited line.

Did he think she was some simpering preteen to be won over by a stud in tight jeans? There was no denying that he wore his jeans with very little room to spare. She was surprised they allowed him to bend down. She couldn't help noticing that. Or the way his muscles had felt, hard and powerful, when he pressed her up against the drywall. And the outline of his body—

Well, never mind his body, she thought, angry with herself for letting her thoughts run off like that. That was exactly what he was hoping for. Just because he was the type of specimen who could make time stand still instead of stopping a clock, he thought that gave him the right to—to—

Preoccupied, she walked into a sawhorse and bumped her shin royally. "Ouch." She jumped back and massaged the tender spot.

Joseph was crossing to her and saw the mishap. It wasn't like Sonny to have an accident. He hurried over. "You okay, Sonny?"

She was embarrassed that someone had witnessed her clumsiness. She stopped massaging and leaned a hip against one of the sawhorse's legs, ignoring the sting in her shin. "Sure, what d'you mean?"

Joseph shrugged. "I don't know. You seem kind of, you know, preoccupied."

Since he had what looked like an order form in his hands, Allison took it from him and tried to gather her thoughts together enough to peruse it. "Just worried that we won't get this extension done in time, that's all."

"That's all?" he echoed.

"Sure." She thrust the unread paper back at him. "What else?"

Joseph scratched his head. "I saw the way Marino looked at you."

She wondered how many others were aware of that, too. "The way Angelo Marino looks at me is his problem, not mine."

Joseph folded the report carefully, running his long, thin fingers along each edge. "How long have we worked together, Sonny?"

"Five years." Joseph had joined the company just after her father had come home from the hospital. She had needed someone she could count on. Joseph had been made-to-order.

He continued smoothing out the edges. "And in that time have you ever known me to butt in where it's none of my business?"

"No." He had been good like that. She smiled at him. The man meant well. But she wasn't in the market for any more well-meant statements about her life. She had all she could handle with Rhonda. "Don't spoil your record, Joseph. You're on a roll."

He had started this, so he doggedly spit it out. "It wouldn't hurt for you to kick back a little. Your father works you too hard. Everyone knows that."

She didn't want people blaming her father for something she did voluntarily. "No, I work me too hard."

Joseph looked at her with eyes that were sympathetic and kind. "What are you trying to prove?"

If it were anyone but Joseph, she wouldn't have even bothered answering. "That I can cut it."

"Don't you think you've already proven that by now?"

She shook her head. Once, she would have thought so, but not anymore. Time had taught her that. There was no rest, no finish line. It just kept getting moved farther ahead. "No, that's something that has to be reestablished with each job. Like this one."

Joseph frowned, his lower lip all but disappearing. "All work and no play make Jill a dull girl."

She patted his arm. It felt almost bony. Not like Angelo's.

She banished the thought from her head. It was bad enough that she had to worry about him popping up physically. He had no place in her head. "I'll worry about Jill," she promised.

Joseph shrugged as he left to take care of the next detail on his list. "Maybe you should start. I would."

"Yes," she whispered to herself, watching him walk off, "but you're not me."

Mercifully Angelo didn't turn up for the remainder of the afternoon to reaffirm his off-the-wall proposal. But the fact that he wasn't there didn't help soothe her frayed nerves. Allison kept looking over her shoulder, expecting him to turn up at any moment. Every time someone approached her from behind she stiffened before turning around. The anticipation was completely doing her in.

But each time she turned around it was someone else trying to get her attention and she breathed a sigh of relief. And felt just a tinge, the slightest twinge of disappointment. But that was only because the threat of his appearing wasn't over, not because she wanted to see him. She definitely didn't want to see him.

It was just that she expected to.

He was making her crazy.

Because time was such a great factor both companies had their crews working long hours and coming in on Saturdays. Sundays were the only days that work beyond the fenced-off area was stilled.

Sunday, she had found, was always a good time to survey in peace and quiet what progress had been made during the week. There were no workers to contend with, no noise.

And no Marino.

She didn't have to be jittery, waiting for him to plant his size-ten boot-shod feet in front of her or anticipating him grabbing her from behind, pressing her body against a wall. Against him. She wouldn't put it past him to pay someone to drop a tool on her from a scaffold just to have an excuse to hold her.

No, that type didn't need excuses, she amended as she brought her car to a stop in the parking lot. He just went ahead and grabbed. She still hadn't gotten an opportunity to talk to his partner about keeping Marino caged or on a leash.

He was making her entirely too nervous. And awakening things inside of her that shouldn't be awakened.

Allison flashed her identification at the guard who was posted on the west end entrance to the site. He waved her on. Nodding at him and pocketing her wallet, Allison walked briskly into the shell of the structure that would house another twenty stores in the not-too-distant future. Right now it looked like the bare ribs of a dinosaur that had knelt on the ground to rest.

She liked this part, liked creating something out of steel and concrete. She had albums of each project Conrad and Son had undertaken, consisting of photographs she had shot of the structure at various stages of completion. This she did on Sundays, as well. That way no one saw this sentimental side of her. It wasn't vanity that prompted her to keep the albums, but pride, pride in her own abilities. It helped ease the pain that overtook her at times. And the loneliness when it came.

She walked in and scanned the empty, cluttered area.

"I was giving up on you. It's about time you showed up."

The deep voice, coming out of nowhere, made her gasp as she jumped back. Looking around quickly, her heart thudding madly against her rib cage, she saw what looked like a picnic table set up on the far side of the floor.

A picnic table with benches and food. And Angelo.

She felt her temper flare. Wasn't she ever going to get any peace from him? She crossed to him, hands on hips, eyes blazing. This was her terrain, damn it. "What are you doing here?"

He spread his hands wide as he remained seated on the tiny bench. "Waiting for you."

"Me?" Didn't the man have a life?

Angelo nodded, gesturing for her to sit down. "Your assistant told me you were going to check out the site today."

Overwhelmed, her knees didn't want to stay solid. She sank down on the other tiny bench that was attached to the table. "Joseph told you?" She thought back to the conversation she had had with Joseph the other day. He thought she needed to kick back a little, but she wouldn't have believed that he'd try to orchestrate an encounter for her.

"Yes."

She stared at him as he poured a glass of wine for her. White. Her favorite. "Why would he tell you that?"

Angelo measured out a glass for himself. "A man does a lot of talking after five beers."

"You got him drunk?" Indignation shook the stunned shock from her. How could he do that to Joseph?

"No, I ran into him after work and offered to buy him a drink. *He* got himself drunk." Angelo saw the look of horror on her face. He didn't have to guess what she was thinking. He knew. Knew a lot about her just by pure instinct. "Don't worry. I drove him home and had someone follow us with his car."

Apparently he was more efficient than she would have given him credit for. "You seem to have gone to an awful lot of trouble."

He broke a piece of bread and buttered it. He'd skipped breakfast to get this all together and was hungry. "Anything worthwhile is worth a lot of effort. Makes the end result that much more precious."

Allison straightened her shoulders. She wasn't going to let herself be flattered by all this. She wasn't. She couldn't help it. Still, she tried to remain firm. "I don't know what you expect to gain—"

He smiled as he passed the bread to her. "Friendship'll do for a starter."

They were going to finish something, not start it. "Marino—"

"I've got lobster." He uncovered the main course for her.

Her appetite stirred. Eating was something she just did to keep alive. But lobster was her one weakness. "Lobster?"

He nodded, raising the platter to her.

The snake tempting Eve in the garden. No, snakes didn't have eyes like this man. Soft, coaxing. Sexy. She wasn't being totally fair, calling him a snake. But then he wasn't being fair, either. She tried to remember if she had ever told Joseph that she liked lobster. "Joseph told you I like lobster?"

"No, Rhonda did."

It was beginning to sound like a conspiracy. "You called my secretary?"

He nodded. "Seemed like the logical thing to do." She was still staring at him as if he had two heads. "It's getting kind of cold, so I think you'd better eat."

Her curiosity was greater than her craving. "Why are you doing this?"

It was obvious, but he explained, anyway. "Well, since Mohammed wouldn't come to the mountain, the mountain pulled up stakes and came instead."

That made absolutely no sense, not that, she was beginning to think, anything he said did. She was still trying to work her way through the "mother of his children" bit. "What?"

He handed her the lobster. "You wouldn't go out with me to have dinner, so I brought dinner to you, or lunch, as it were."

She had thought she had his number. Now she wasn't so sure. What if she hadn't come? "You went to all this trouble to have lunch with me?"

"Yes."

"Why?" she repeated the question again. So far she hadn't heard anything that explained this to her satisfaction.

He knew half a dozen women who would have loved to have been wined and dined in such a whimsically romantic fashion. But not her.

Maybe that was where the attraction lay, he mused. She was unique. "You ask an awful lot of questions for a woman with an empty stomach."

"And I'm not getting any answers. What is it you want? And don't," she put in quickly, "tell me friendship."

Dottie had packed cold macaroni salad as a side dish. He urged it on Allison now. It was Dottie who had put all this together for him this morning, talking on about how sweet he had been to send flowers and asking question after question about Allison. Everyone was in his corner. Everyone but Allison. "Well, you didn't like my suggesting you be the mother of my children, so I thought we'd go another route for a while."

She took the salad, debating whether to eat it or dump it on his head. She hated waste, so she ate it. "You're being absurd."

He waited a beat before he said anything, letting her enjoy the food. Letting himself enjoy the sight of her. "Why? Hasn't anyone ever told you that they wanted you?"

She raised her eyes to his, placing the fork on the dish. She had been right all along, after all. He'd had her going there for a minute. "So that's what this is all about. A tumble in the hay."

"We've already tumbled," he answered innocently, "and it wasn't hay. It was grass."

He was doing this deliberately. She sipped the wine to fortify herself and suddenly realized that she had emptied her glass. "Why are you trying to drive me crazy?"

"I'm not trying to drive you crazy, Allison. I'm trying to get you to relax a little with me." He refilled her glass.

She eyed the shimmering wine. He hadn't brought plastic cups. These were cut glass. The man had style. And too much tenacity. She didn't want to be worn down. "You're trying to get me drunk."

"That'll come later." He grinned as he shook his head in response to the wary look on her face. "It was a joke. I don't want you blaming your actions on anything else but your own free will."

"If I followed my own free will, Marino, you wouldn't like it." It was meant as a threat. It was made out of fear. Not that he would do something to her here, but that she was doing something to herself, just by being here with him. Her confidence was getting seriously shaken. There was something almost attractive about all this. Seductive. God, he was seductive. But she wasn't going to give in to a momentary tug of nature.

His lips spread wide. The man's mouth was far too sensual. She wondered if it was the wine that was affecting her. At least she could hope so.

"Try me."

She tried to make sense out of what he was saying. Things seemed to be traveling through her mind in a jumbled manner. "Are you one of those?"

"One of what?"

She shrugged, frustrated, searching for words, wishing her mind was clearer. She shouldn't have had the wine so quickly. And on an empty stomach. There was an apple in her bag that was supposed to serve as lunch. "You said free will. Are you the type of person who's into chains and things?"

"I'm not into physical ones, only spiritual ones—the good kind."

She looked down on the table. How did his hand get there on top of hers? She didn't remember that happening. She tried to move it away, but it was trapped. She was trapped. "What do you mean by that?"

"There are chains that bind and shackle you," he said easily, stroking a thumb over her hand, watching her try to hold back a shiver, "rather than the good ones that make you feel secure, a part of something. A willing part."

She swallowed, her mouth suddenly dry. "I don't follow you," she lied. That was the trouble. She followed him all too well.

"I think you don't want to follow me."

She began to rise. His hold on her hand tightened just a little. She leveled an accusing look at him. It was supposed to make him back off. He didn't. "I can scream. The guard'll come."

She was afraid. He could see it. It was like trying to gain the confidence of a child who had been mistreated, or an animal that had been beaten. Was she that distrustful of love? Who had hurt her this way? "The guard is five feet tall and on retirement. I could press him over my head if I wanted to." His eyes coaxed her to sit and relax. "I'd rather sit here and eat with you. Talk to me, Allison. Don't spar, even though I like the feisty look in your eyes." He saw the beginning of a smile on her lips. "Talk to me."

"About what?" she asked guardedly.

"Anything but construction and this extension."

"Construction is all I know," she answered stubbornly, refusing to let him into her inner soul.

His eyes skimmed over her face, touching it lightly. She could almost feel him. "Someone as beautiful as you should know a lot more that just that."

She raised her chin. "I'm proud of my work."

He'd wait her out. "That's good, but it shouldn't be your entire life."

He was passing judgment again, and she resented it, even if what he said was true. That just made it worse. "You don't know anything about my life."

"Then tell me."

She looked down at her plate, her appetite waning. "I don't make a habit of exposing my inner thoughts to strangers."

She wasn't going to shut him out. "People are only strangers if you want them to be."

She looked at him meaningfully. He was finally getting the message. "Right."

He laughed, retreating for only a moment. "You're a hard nut to crack."

She relaxed just a fraction. "I'm an impossible nut to crack, Marino."

He took a healthy bite of his lobster. "Nothing is impossible if you want it badly enough."

She felt as if he was putting her on notice. Ignoring him, she turned her attention to her lunch. That at least she could understand. "Eat your lobster," she muttered, keeping her eyes on her own plate.

Chapter Seven

Angelo watched Allison eat for several moments in silence. The way he saw it the lady needed a little more persuading to tip the scales in his favor She needed to be shown what he in his heart already knew "Tell me, Allison, are you up to a test?"

She was certain that the lobster was delicious, but she hadn't tasted a single bite of her meal since she had started eating. She was too busy dealing with the way her body was rebelling against her, reacting to being so close to him. She regarded him warily. "What sort of test?"

His mouth seemed to tease hers as he smiled at her invitingly "Kiss me."

Stunned, Allison felt her fork slip from her fingers. It fell to the plate with a clatter The noise jarred her back to her senses. "Now I know you're crazy."

He moved her dish aside and took her hands in his. Her fingers felt icy. "Afraid?"

Why did he keep having this effect on her? He was ruining her carefully constructed facade. "Of a certifiably crazy person? Yes.'' Nerves played leapfrog all through her as the look on his face became serious.

She had to be made to understand. Angelo was going to make her an offer he knew she couldn't refuse. He was risking everything on it. But he was playing to win. ''Kiss me, and if you don't feel anything, I'll fold my picnic table and disappear into the night forever.''

Kiss him? She drew her eyes away from his mouth, realizing that her breath had grown shorter. All right, she was tempted, she admitted that, if only to herself. But she wasn't free to let herself go like this. ''Not that seeing you retreat isn't a tempting offer, but I don't see how kissing you is going to solve anything.''

He saw beyond her words to the flicker of fear in her eyes. She was afraid to find out that she liked him. That she was attracted to him and that they had a future together. He was going to have to show her the way. ''You *are* afraid.''

She threw down the napkin and rose awkwardly from the bench. It caught the hem of her slacks and she tugged herself loose. Her action reminded him a little of a frightened animal trying to elude a trap. ''And you are obnoxious, overbearing and impossible.'' Free, she began to hurry away. The hell with taking stock of the work. She'd do it tomorrow. Now all she wanted to do was get away from him and his proposal.

She couldn't just walk away from this. He wouldn't let her. ''Admit it, you like me, don't you?'' He matched her step for step to the exit.

Allison kept walking, her stride long and measured. And quick. She couldn't shake him. ''I'm bringing my dog to work from now on.'' *And possibly a gun.*

He was nothing if not persistent and he wasn't about to lose her, not when he felt he was close. ''One kiss and you won't have to.''

The situation suddenly dawned on her. What was she doing, running? She never ran. She faced things, no matter how unpleasant. She always had. What was he *doing* to her?

She stopped so abruptly that she took him completely by surprise. Angelo came to a skidding halt in order not to bump into her. Muttering an oath under her breath, she quickly turned and brushed her lips against his, then all but jumped back, as if she'd touched a live wire. In a way it felt as if she had. But she wasn't about to admit it to him.

"There, nothing." She pointed to the table behind them. "Fold and go."

To her distress he didn't appear to be going anywhere. "I said a kiss."

She placed her hands on her hips. She might have known he'd renege. "That *was* a kiss."

The grin was slow and sexy and bunched her stomach into a huge knot that refused to dissolve. "Oh, lady, you don't know what you've been missing."

Allison began walking away again. It was an instinctive move deeply tied to self-preservation. "A gun permit comes to mind."

"It's hard to kiss a moving target, Allison. Are you going to stand still, or do I have to throw a rope over you and tie you up?"

Allison swung around, throwing up her hands. "All right, all right! Let's get this over with."

How bad could it be? Like a gladiator marching into the arena, she squared her shoulders and tilted her face up, braced, waiting. It annoyed her that she realized she was rubbing her thumb over her forefinger so hard that the skin hurt.

Her eyes were opened. "You're going to watch?" he asked, surprised.

She gritted her teeth together. "Every last move."

He only grinned. But instead of lowering his mouth to hers he slowly slipped his fingers into her hair, framing her

...LAY

...OUETTE'S

...HEARTS

...ME

...D GET

- ...REE BOOKS
- ...REE "KEY TO YOUR HEART" ...ENDANT NECKLACE
- ...REE SURPRISE GIFT
- ...ND MUCH MORE

...THE PAGE AND
...YOURSELF IN →

PLAY "LUCKY H
AND GET . . .

★ **Exciting Silhouette Romance™ n**
★ **"Key to Your Heart" pendant ne**
★ **Surprise mystery gift that will d**

THEN CONTINUE
LUCKY STREAK V
SWEETHEART OF

When you return the postcard on
send you the books and gifts you
free! Then, you'll get 6 new Silho
every month, delivered right to yo
they're available in stores. If you
you'll pay only $1.99* each plus 2
applicable sales tax, if any*. That
and—compared to cover prices of
quite a bargain!

Free Newsletter!

You'll get our subscribers-only ne
look at our most popular authors
novels.

Special Extras—Free!

When you join the Silhouette Rea
also get additional free gifts from
of our appreciation for being a ho

*Terms and prices subject to change without notice
Sales tax applicable in N.Y.

face. She deliberately ignored the quick, sharp foreshadowing that jangled her nerves. It was only through effort that she didn't take in the deep, steadying breath she suddenly found herself needing. She felt her insides vibrating like a jackhammer.

"Is this going to take long?" she asked in a voice she didn't recognize. There was a slight quake in it. She wasn't accustomed to that. Nor to the sudden rush of desire that came over her. "I still have work to do."

He didn't answer. He just stared at her, desire mingling with reverence in his eyes. Her pulse scrambled, sending a message to her system. The tattoo spelled out Mayday except that she wasn't up to unscrambling it. It was all she could do to keep from bolting again.

"It'll be over," he told her, the soft words whispering seductively across her lips, making them part, "when it's over."

Anger, her only shield, was showing cracks like a poorly poured foundation. "Brilliant statement. Are you trying to live up to Yogi Berra's wit?" Those were the words she thought she'd said, but maybe she hadn't. Maybe she only thought them in her mind. She couldn't seem to get anything past her throat. Something was blocking it. There was a wild, hammering pulse in the way.

He saw the slight tremor of her throat, saw the flare of something in her eyes. Desire. He recognized it before she banked it down. So she wasn't quite as immune to him as she was trying to pretend. It was all the encouragement he needed.

With aching restraint he touched his lips to hers ever so lightly. Her lips parted involuntarily in response. She closed her eyes and moved toward him against her will.

Just a second ago she wanted this over with. Now, now she didn't know what she wanted. More. She wanted more. No, that couldn't be right. This wasn't acceptable. It had to stop, before she became any further unstrung by this construction saboteur.

But when his lips finally came in contact with hers, the tension was so great that she felt as if a rubber band had snapped within her. Snapped, allowing everything that she was holding so tightly together to burst, fanning out all through her.

His mouth tasted of something warm, tangy and deeply male. Without meaning to she ran her tongue along his lips and heard him groan as he tightened his hold on her. She could feel each one of his fingers as he slid them along her back, pressing her into him.

In the far recesses of her mind she'd wondered what it would be like to kiss him ever since Fate had flung her onto Angelo's body.

Now she knew.

It was like plummeting down a roller coaster incline without the roller coaster offering her any safety. Air refused to enter her lungs, held at bay by the thudding of her heart.

She gripped his forearms. She was shoving him away. At least she thought she was. But if that was true, why was she holding on to his sleeves so tightly, bunching the material beneath her fingers?

He bracketed her face again, his mouth slanting over hers, draining, replenishing, losing himself in the gift he wanted to give her. He wanted to prove something to her, to show her that she was affected by him. He hadn't given a thought to the possibility of his falling into a trap himself, at least not this completely. Kissing her was like spinning into a vortex. Time, space, dimensions, none of these had any meaning for him. Everything around him had either stood still or just faded away. All he was aware of was the fact that her mouth was sweet and that he ached for her. If she was a wish before, now she was almost an obsession, a craving so deep that he felt his life would end if he couldn't have her.

His hands had slipped from her face, down the length of her sides to her waist. His fingers ached to touch her, to encompass the soft flesh of her breasts slowly until his skin burned. But that was going too fast, too soon. He'd frighten her away. Angelo knew he'd have to wait. He encircled her waist and held her close.

But even that was too dangerous. If he didn't stop now, he would undo everything he had painstakingly accomplished so far.

When he drew away, she tottered slightly, grasping his arms harder to regain her balance. Her head was still spinning. She had always thought of that description as some absurd fabrication by an overly romantic observer. Now she knew it was true. At least with Angelo.

She blinked several times, realizing that she had indeed shut her eyes. Allison grasped at straws, a drowning woman trying to find salvation. That was it—she'd closed her eyes and lost her equilibrium. Inner ear infections did that to you. And she had an infection. She raised her eyes to Angelo's rugged face.

A bad one.

"Well?" He loosened his hold on her waist but still rested his hands on the tempting swell of her hips. He couldn't wean himself from the feel of her in one step. It wasn't that easy.

It took Allison a moment before she felt capable of speaking coherently. "Fold your table."

His eyes held hers. Oh, no, she wasn't going to get away with it. "You're not going to tell me you didn't feel anything?"

She took a deep, guarded breath. How long before her pulse would return to normal? How long before her legs felt sturdy again? "I'm not?"

He shook his head slowly. "No, you're not the type to lie."

She swallowed. The dryness wouldn't go away. It persisted, the way it did if she had had too much wine. Or too much Angelo. "What makes you think I'd be lying?"

He touched the tip of his tongue to his forefinger and then slowly ran it along her bottom lip. He watched it quiver involuntarily, making desire shoot twin shafts, hitting the mark with both of them. "You forget, I was there."

God, she did want to kiss him again. But that would be the worst thing she could do. "You're an egotist."

"Not this time." He tried to recall if he had ever felt even remotely like this about a woman. "Actually, not ever," he murmured out loud. "I can give you references."

Now he was flaunting his other women. "I'll just bet you can."

He found he could read her mind. She had misunderstood and was jealous. He liked that. It meant she did care, even if she didn't know it, or wouldn't admit it. "From my family. They'll tell you I'm a very unassuming guy."

She relaxed, but only a little. She realized that she was still standing there, letting him hold her. Enjoying it. She took his hands from her waist and pushed them aside, but not as forcefully as she would have just a few minutes ago. "Unassuming guys don't stalk."

She didn't sound as adamant as before. He congratulated himself on gaining ground. "Neither do I. But I do want you."

There was something in his eyes that made her believe he was serious, even while logically she knew it had to be ridiculous.

No, it was more than his eyes; it had been there in his kiss, just like the old song had predicted. When she agreed to let him kiss her, she had expected roughness, to be stormed like a fortress by a plundering Viking. She hadn't been prepared for the sweetness, for the gentle way in which his kiss had unraveled her by layers, by degrees, until it had left her mindless, without a will of her own.

Love's first kiss.

My God, what was she thinking? She was letting herself get carried away and there was no place for her to be carried to, no place to go. She knew that. It was a simple, hard fact of life. Everyone was alone. There wasn't any such thing as love. Not really. Only an illusion that left at dawn's early light. Life was hard. One had to be even harder to survive. Her father had taught her that in more ways than one.

She crossed to the table. In the confusion she had left her purse behind. She picked it up and clutched the strap in her hands. Maybe she could still appeal to his sense of decency. "Look, I'm not like the other women you're probably used to."

Now that he had kissed her he found himself wanting to do it again and again. He satisfied himself by toying with a springy curl that lay against her cheek. He watched in fascination as her cheek trembled slightly beneath his touch. "I'll be the first to agree to that."

He was playing word games with her. "Marino, I have responsibilities, duties, things you don't seem to understand."

He was tired of the role she cast him in without stopping to verify if it was true. "That wasn't fair. You're judging me without anything to base it on and you know it." He reached for her hand, but she took a step away, eluding him. "I come from a very close-knit family where responsibility is a hallmark. It's part of loving. When you love, you feel responsible and you take action upon that responsibility. It goes hand in hand." He had always been there for his family, even when they didn't realize they wanted him to be. That, too, was part of loving. He was there for her if she would only stop being afraid and see.

She thought of herself, of the way her father regarded her despite all her efforts. No matter how much she tried to please him, how much she put into the relationship, nothing came out. The only time she ever saw any results from her efforts was when she was constructing something. Structures, not relationships, worked for her.

"Not always. Sometimes one can exist without the other." She struggled not to cry. What had kissing Angelo unlocked inside of her? She was usually so self-possessed. No one saw this side of her. No one. No one knew about the needy girl that existed within the poised woman. Damn him, why didn't he leave her be? "Sometimes you can be responsible without a single shred of love coming into the picture."

He wanted nothing more than to have her share her burdens with him, to have her know that he would always be there to help. "Tell me about the picture, Allison."

She was tempted. For whatever reason she was tempted to tell him, to let the hurt spill out once and for all. Maybe she had carried the pain of rejection, of never being good enough for her father around with her for too long. Maybe she just needed human contact. Or maybe the tenderness in his kiss had disarmed her.

But she couldn't tell him. Years of keeping everything inside were hard to overcome in a few short moments, even if she wanted to. Even if she admitted to wanting to.

Instead, Allison directed his attention to something she thought he'd see as a minor point, although it wasn't to her "Everyone else calls me Sonny."

He touched her face with the back of his hand, watching her eyes grow smoky with anticipation even as the rest of her stiffened. "I don't want to be like everyone else in your life, Allison."

This wasn't going to lead anywhere. It couldn't. She pulled herself away from the drugging influence of his touch. "I have work to do, Angelo, and I'd appreciate you letting me do it."

She had called him by his first name. Another small step forward. He could only push so far at one time and he knew it. He nodded. "Okay." Trying to seem nonchalant, he placed the plates into the basket. Dottie would have a fit if he forgot them. The whole thing belonged to her. "Mind if I tag along?"

As if she had any say in the matter. "Would you stay here if I told you to?"

He grinned. They both knew the answer to that one. "No, but I thought it would be polite to give you a chance to say yes."

She laughed and shook her head. He was utterly impossible. But she wasn't finding that as offensive as she had. She thought back to her original assessment of his capabilities. "I suppose I should be grateful that you're not grabbing me by my hair and trying to drag me into your lair."

He tucked the tablecloth over the wares in the basket. He was tidy. The fact surprised and oddly pleased her. "Not my style. Besides, I don't have a lair. I do have a nice three-bedroom house that I'd like to show you sometime."

Wasn't there a line that went with that sort of invitation? She remembered. "What, no etchings?" Amusement was in her eyes.

Yes, there was definite progress here. He'd have to be careful not to jeopardize it. "I could buy some if you'd like."

She laughed. "You're crazy." This time it wasn't an accusation.

"There's been some talk of that." *Crazy about you,* he added silently.

Effortlessly he slipped his arm around her shoulders, and she stiffened for just a moment. He waited for her to shrug him off. Instead, he saw her take a breath and make a conscious effort to relax.

Score one for the home team, he thought with a smile he wisely kept to himself.

There was no use in fighting him off, Allison thought as they walked through the huge structure and she attempted to do what usually came so naturally to her. Having his arm around her shoulders was a harmless enough gesture, and she supposed in his own way that Angelo Marino was harmless, too.

No, that wasn't true, either. He wasn't that and she knew it. Harmless men didn't make everything inside of you feel as if it were in a blender being mixed at high speed when they kissed you.

But there would be no occasion for him to kiss her again, and if she remained guardedly friendly, maybe he wouldn't feel compelled to try to storm her ramparts again. Some men, she knew, lived for a challenge, and if she fought too hard, it might goad him to try harder. She'd be friendly, complacent, and then he'd go away.

It was a nice philosophy. She thought it might even have a chance of working. What she didn't understand was why she couldn't bring herself to cheer it on wholeheartedly.

He knew a lot about the business, she realized later. That meant the success of his company wasn't entirely due to his partner's capabilities. Angelo was astute. Very astute. He just didn't believe in showing off.

As they reviewed the progress of the past week together, he casually mentioned a few shortcuts to her that made good monetary sense without undermining the integrity of the work. Relief overwhelmed her more than it should have when she learned that he didn't believe in shoddy work. In his own, unassuming way he was as proud of his work as she of hers. But she wore her accomplishments like a badge, a testimony of her self-worth. To him his were merely a natural extension of himself. No big deal.

She'd never met anyone like him.

On Monday mornings she and Shad and Angelo met regularly in the crammed construction site trailer to compare notes and see how far progress was going and how well. Problems were dissected and solutions were discussed. For the first time she began to feel part of a larger team. More important, she didn't feel as though everything was resting exclusively on her shoulders. It seemed ironic, since their company was so much smaller than hers. Used to exercising total control over everything, the teamwork took a bit of effort on her part, but it was well worth it.

The wings of the extension were continuing to go up in tandem. Angelo made it clear to her that they didn't want to face the penalty clause any more than she did. To her it was a matter of prestige. To them it was the cold hard dollar that made going over the time limit doubly undesirable.

Her apprehensions began to dissolve.

"Well, I guess that's all for now," Shad said as he broke up another meeting. "Unless either of you have anything else to add or go over." He looked from one to the other.

She shook her head, rising from the makeshift table that reminded her of the picnic table Angelo had set up the day before.

Someone knocked on the door and then peered in. Angelo was needed in another section. Reluctantly Angelo took his leave, but he caught her eye just before he walked out.

Allison looked away first. There was something there, in his eyes. A promise, warmth, a lot of things she couldn't let herself believe in. If she did, it would spoil everything. It would break her resolve, all those years of carefully building up her defenses. He had almost undone her yesterday. That couldn't be allowed to happen again no matter how much she had enjoyed it.

She hesitated, looking at Shad as he gathered some notes together. Now or never. "Mr. McClellan, I'd like to talk to you." She glanced at Angelo's retreating back as he left the trailer and moistened her lips. "Alone."

He smiled at her, trying to put her at her ease. She looked tense again. Uncomfortable. "You might find it easier to talk to me if you called me Shad." He watched as she ran her tongue along her lips again. Yes, he could see why Angelo had fallen so hard. She was a beautiful woman. But he had yet to be convinced that the beauty went on to where it counted—inside. He gestured to her chair again, waiting until she sat down before he took a seat. "This is about Angelo, isn't it?"

"Yes." She breathed the answer, relieved that she didn't have to find a way to broach the subject. "Can you call him off?"

Did she think it was that easy? "He's not my pet German shepherd, Ms. Conrad."

"Sonny," she corrected mechanically. She found she admired Shad too much to continue being addressed so formally. She folded her hands in front of her. "I know, but you're his partner and I thought he might listen to you." She began to fold and unfold a piece of notepaper on her pad.

"I'm more than that. I'm his brother. But he still won't listen. And besides," he added kindly, but firmly, "I wouldn't presume to tell him what to do."

She stared at Shad. He and Angelo didn't look a thing alike despite their dark coloring. Angelo's features were blunter, broader, more powerful. The planes of Shad's face were more aristocratic and angular. "His brother? I'm sorry. Your names are different and I thought—"

Shad came to her rescue. "He's my foster brother if you want to be exact. His family took my sister Dottie and me in over twenty years ago. We grew up together. I think I know him better than anyone on earth, and when Angelo makes up his mind about something, I'm not even sure God can make him change it."

She drew in an unsettled breath. She didn't want to be the object of someone's attention. It made her feel too vulnerable. It made her dream. And dreams weren't real. "Don't I get a say in it?"

Shad studied her for a moment. There were things about Allison that reminded him of J.T., the way she was before she let her barriers drop. "I think you've already had your say."

She looked at him sharply. Had Angelo bragged about yesterday, about how easily she had melted into his kiss? "What are you talking about?"

He had noticed the way she was fidgeting when she talked. It wasn't a case of her not liking Angelo, he'd guess. It was a case of her being afraid to like him. He had seen the way she had looked at his brother this morning when she thought no one noticed. He had seen the way she seemed to come to attention when Angelo talked. "Ever read Shakespeare, Sonny?"

What did that have to do with anything? "Yes, of course." She shrugged, remembering a tedious course. "High school. A little in college, but I don't see—"

"Do you remember that line about 'the lady doth protest too much?'"

"The lady," she corrected, rising, "is not protesting. She's just not interested." She should have known she'd get no help in this quarter. She was back to trying to fight this on her own. And the problem was, her weapons were getting extremely dull. "I thought you were the sensible one."

Shad took no offense as he got to his feet. "I am."

How could he believe that? "You're sticking up for him."

He smiled. "Families do that."

She sighed. The whole family was crazy, she thought. Supportive and crazy. She walked away, wondering what it would have been like to have grown up part of a family like his, instead of rich and alone.

Chapter Eight

The following Friday Allison wandered through the maze of spools of electrical wiring, frowning deeply. Everywhere she looked in the area set aside for deliveries it was the same. "These aren't acceptable, Joseph." She ran her hand down one huge spool. "They're not the right gauge."

Joseph had hurried to bring this to her attention as soon as he had checked the latest shipment. "Yeah, I know. I hear that's what they said, too."

She wanted to shove the spool aside in her frustration but held the impulse in check. It was too heavy for her to move, and fits of temper never solved anything, anyway. If this wasn't resolved quickly, it was going to put them behind. Their margin of time was evaporating. She turned and looked at Joseph as his words suddenly dawned on her. "They?"

"Marino and McClellan." He nodded in the general direction of the east wing. "The contractors from hell, I think you called them."

That had been during the first week. Nerves and temper had brought that on. It was another story now. "I know what I called them." She bit her lip, thinking over her options. "I didn't know they were using the same subcontractor."

"Miller and Jones are the largest."

Yes, she knew that. "And it looks as if they want to get even larger by cutting corners." One length of wire had loosened from one of the spools and lay on the ground like a long, dark snake. She kicked it out of the way. "I won't use this. It's substandard, and I'm not taking chances on something happening two, five, ten years down the line because it was simpler to let things slide than to go back and demand wiring that's up to code." Thinking of a barrage of names that Harley Miller, Jr., deserved for doing something so underhanded, Allison reached for her phone.

Joseph shook his head, stopping her. "I already tried that. He's going to be in meetings all day and can't be reached."

"Meetings," she echoed. "At his office?"

"So the secretary said."

She made up her mind. Miller was going to deliver and use the right wiring, or she was going to stuff this wire down his throat. "Well, he's going to be in for another meeting he hadn't planned on when he went over his agenda today." She handed Joseph her phone as she ran her hands through her hair. She wasn't exactly dressed for a meeting in her jeans and work shirt, but that wasn't going to stop her. Not when time was at stake.

Joseph juggled the phone with his clipboard. "You're going to see him?"

Allison's eyes narrowed. She thought of Harley Miller, Jr., soft, pudgy, with a round, sweaty little face set on top of a round, sweaty little body. He was the type of man who thought money could buy everything. Including, it appeared, cooperation. He wasn't half the man his father had been. She wondered how his partner put up with him. Integrity had always been a byword with Henry Jones.

"Fastest way I know to get this thing resolved," she said. "Ever since he took over his father's place in the business, he's been trying to find a way to turn a bigger profit. Well, he's not going to do it by installing the wrong wiring in any of my buildings."

"Smile when you say that, partner."

She whirled around, knowing before she looked that Angelo was standing there. It was almost three. She had been expecting him to show up all day. Waiting for him, really. He would come at just the worst possible time. She was fit to be tied over this. His poking fun at her didn't help. "It's not funny."

Angelo and Shad had just finished a discussion about the electrical wire they had received. Angelo had come to see what she thought about the matter. "No," he said seriously, "it's not. It's very *un*funny. I take it you're going to go see him."

"Yes." At the moment nothing would have given her greater pleasure than to see Harley Miller, Jr., tarred and feathered and bound with his own wiring. She couldn't abide anyone who tried to cheat.

She was really something to look at when her honor was at stake, he thought. There was a flash in her eyes that bordered on dangerous. He hooked his thumbs into his jeans. "Want company?"

She looked at Angelo as she picked up a length of wire that Joseph had cut to examine more closely. Did he think she was incapable of handling this on her own? "I don't need anyone to hold my hand."

Angelo had already told Shad he was going to go and corner Miller after he couldn't be reached by phone. Going with Allison was a bonus. "Everyone needs someone to hold their hand once in a while. I was thinking more in terms of you holding mine."

She eyed him suspiciously. "I don't have time to fight off another pass."

"Fine." He ushered her toward the narrow corridor formed by plywood fences running parallel to each other and feeding into the entrance of the actual mall. "Then don't fight."

She opened her mouth to put him in his place. She was so annoyed with Miller that she didn't realize just where Angelo had led her until it was too late. Allison looked around now and pulled her hand away.

Before she knew it, just as she anticipated it, he pulled her into his arms and kissed her. Kissed her until she was breathless and miles past the point where she could fight him off. Far beyond the point where she wanted to.

Ecstasy, fright, joy, anger, desire, all came in a flood, rushing into her and dragging her beneath them even as they buoyed her up. The kiss was rougher than it had been last time, more primitive in its demands and yearnings, but no less stunning.

Allison held on for the ride, intent on giving as good as she got, desperately wanting to share this rush, to make him as much a prisoner of all this as she was. It wasn't fair if it was all one-sided. Even in its beauty it trapped her, and if she was going to be trapped, it wasn't going to be alone.

Angelo had always prided himself on being able to hold his own when it came to drinking. No whiskey, no amount of alcohol was half as potent as she was. He felt utterly drunk on her kiss. Utterly intoxicated with her.

His breath short, his pulse racing, he knew he'd never satisfy himself, and now was no time even to try to get his fill of her. But he had needed that. He smiled into her face.

"I've been dying to do that for a whole week." He grinned as he released her. "I don't think I'm going to be able to go that long between refills again." She started to say something, but he wouldn't let her get in a word. "Now then, I'm coming with you, Allison, whether you like it or not. We don't take kindly to anyone who tries to put something over on us. Besides," he added, "I like thinking we're on the same side. Humor me."

"All right." She blew out a breath as she turned to walk out. "You can come." Not that, she knew, she'd be able to stop him if he wanted to accompany her. But she just wanted him to know it wasn't against her will. And though she was perfectly capable of resolving this on her own, did she welcome the fact that she wasn't shouldering everything alone?

They walked briskly to the parking lot. Without thinking she approached her car, then looked back at him. Was he coming with her, or on his own? "Are you going to drive, too?"

He shook his head. "Seems a shame to bring two cars to the same place, pollution and all that. Car pooling is the wave of the future."

If he ever got out of the construction business, he could always be a used car salesman, she thought. The man could really pitch. She gestured toward the passenger side as she hit the door release button. "Get in."

A lazy smile flitted over his tanned face. "Why, Allison, I thought you'd never ask."

She ignored him.

As she drove onto the on ramp of the San Diego Freeway, Allison ran her tongue over her lower lip, then stopped when she realized what she was doing. Her lips still tingled from the impression of his mouth. Not only that, but his presence in the car was almost overwhelming, even though he was just fiddling with the radio dial, not saying anything. He knew what he was doing to her. Damn him, anyway, what right did he have to come barging into her life, throwing it into chaos?

She looked at him as he found a station that apparently satisfied him and leaned back. "Why are you doing this to me?"

"Doing what?" He turned his eyes toward her, and even though she was watching the road, she could feel them. "What am I doing to you?"

His voice was low and sexy, and her hands grew damp as she clutched the steering wheel. It was past the time for denial. She needed the truth if she hoped to survive this. "Trying to mess with my mind." A car cut in front of her, and she hardly had time to step on the brakes. The tires screeched as she slowed down, then evened out. "Ruining my concentration." She let out a breath as the car in front of her speeded up.

Despite what she thought, it wasn't his ego that was pleased by her grudging admission. It was his heart. "Am I? Am I doing that to you?"

She gritted her teeth. She wouldn't have admitted this for the world, but she needed answers. "You know you are."

"Maybe if you didn't fight it so hard," he suggested softly.

She didn't like the way his voice was getting under her skin. She didn't want to weaken this way. The weak were walked on. Sometimes it even happened when you were strong. "What 'it'?" she demanded sharply.

He watched the color come into her cheeks as she waged her own internal battle with what he said. "This attraction between us."

"There is no attraction." At least none that she would admit to out loud. It was bad enough admitting it to herself.

For an engineer she was certainly not being logical, Angelo thought. "If there wasn't, I wouldn't be messing up your concentration." He saw her give him a damning side glance. "To quote you," he added.

Maybe if she gave him this, he'd leave it alone. "All right." She took a breath. "There's attraction."

It was more than he thought she'd concede. "And there'll be more than that in time for you." He watched her jaw tighten. With his eyes closed he could conjure her up perfectly in his mind. He had memorized every contour, every curve, every taste. He reached out and curled a strand of her hair around his finger, savoring the texture. "There already is for me."

She wasn't going to let him get to her, not like this. She fought back, armed with fear. Suddenly she felt frightened, frightened of the feeling she had, frightened of what lay out there for her. "Is this the way you wear down the women you go out with?"

Just the touch of her hair made him want more. To touch her face, her arms, her body. He wanted her, and it was hard to sit here and talk so calmly when all of him felt on fire. "I haven't gone out with that many women and I've never had to 'wear any of them down,' as you put it." Lightly he played his fingertips along her neck, just barely touching her skin.

It was all she could do to keep from shutting her eyes. He was playing havoc with her insides again, making them quiver. Making her want. "Then this is something new to you." She tried to sound sarcastic.

He thought of the way she made him feel. "Oh, yeah," he said heartily.

"Will you stop playing with my hair and my neck and my everything!" she demanded.

"Sorry." He dropped his hand. "It's just that I like the feel of your hair. I like the feel of you."

"Don't." It was almost a plea. She hated the sound of that. She had never pleaded for anything before. Pleas didn't get answered.

But he shook his head solemnly. "That's not something I have much of a say-so in." He shifted slightly, moving the seat belt aside so he could really look at her. "Why are you afraid to feel something, Allison?"

For a second she had almost forgotten what a pompous ass he was. "I'm not afraid to feel."

The contradiction came easily, dressed in a gentle, knowing voice and all the more aggravating for it. "Yes, you are."

"God, but you're infuriating." Why did she have to spell it out for him? Couldn't he just read between the lines and stop harassing her? Stop popping up in her dreams, tempting her with that lethal mouth of his? "Look, I'm not free to feel like other women are, okay? I made a promise."

He knew if he stopped here, she wouldn't explain what she was talking about. He'd have to goad it out of her. "Nuns make promises not to feel like other women do. You don't look like a nun to me."

His voice was gentle, coaxing. He was disintegrating her walls. She could have punched his lights out if her hands weren't otherwise occupied.

"And even nuns change their minds. God lets them out of their bargain."

He was rubbing the back of her neck again, and she fervently wished he'd stop. "Well, He won't let me out of this one."

He stopped and stared at her. "You made a bargain with God?"

She shouldn't have admitted that. No one knew about that. Allison could have bitten off her tongue. "Sort of."

He tried to picture it and found he couldn't. What could she have possibly wanted so badly that she had to bargain with God rather than rely on her own resources? It didn't sound like her. "What kind of bargain?"

She'd gone this far; she might as well tell him the rest of it. "That if He let my father live, I'd stay on, work at the company, devote myself to my father..."

Her voice trailed off. The long, agonizing hours in the hospital corridor, not knowing if her father would live or die, came back to her and she shivered. She felt her throat tighten as she looked ahead, remembering the accident, remembering the car that had come from nowhere, crashing into them. Her father's scream. She felt tears sting her eyes. "It was my fault, anyway."

"Pull over."

Her head cleared as his voice, deep and commanding, registered. "What?"

"I said, pull over." He had one hand on the wheel to reinforce his words. "You're in no condition to drive and talk at the same time, not about this."

Who did he think he was, telling her what to do? "Then I'll stop talking. I don't know what came over me—"

Oh, no, she'd gone past the point of no return. "You need to get the rest of this out." He looked to see if the shoulder of the road was accessible. "You can pull over here."

Her temper, fueled by her embarrassment of exposing herself so blatantly, flared. "Who the hell are you to tell me what I need—?"

He placed his hand on top of hers on the wheel and gently pulled to the right. "Someone who cares."

She resisted, straightening the wheel. "Oh, just like that?"

He made no effort to move the wheel again, but he didn't withdraw his hand. "Yes, just like that."

Tears, damn it, tears were forming. They'd start to flow any second now. She cursed him for that as she pulled onto the shoulder of the freeway. She blinked furiously to keep them back. "I don't need anyone to care about me."

"The hell you don't." Despite the bucket seat he leaned over and slipped an arm around her shoulders. He wanted to be her friend as well as her lover. "Everyone needs someone. Isolation distorts your perspective. You need to interface with someone who cares. Like me. Now talk to me, or we'll stay here all day and all night if we have to." With his free hand he pulled the keys out of the ignition and curved his fingers around them.

She pulled away from him as far as she could in the limited, confining space. "You can't keep me in this car. We have business to attend to."

He sighed and fought for patience. He won. "I don't care about anything but you at this moment. And in case you haven't noticed, I'm a lot bigger than you are."

Allison folded her hands in her lap and stared straight ahead at the traffic that was whizzing by. Angelo was certain she had decided to employ silent resistance, but then, in an almost emotionless voice, she started to speak.

He might as well have all of it. She knew him well enough by now to know that if nothing else, the man was persistent. She thought back to last Sunday. Allison knew he'd wait her out.

"I was five years old when my mother died. My father doesn't talk about her at all. I could never understand that, to have had a wife and never mention her, as if she hadn't existed." She ran her finger along the steering wheel. "One day she was in my life, holding my hand, making things beautiful. The next, she was in the hospital."

Allison closed her eyes, but the tears slipped through her lashes. All these years and she still grieved over the waste of such a young life. And over her own loss. "And then she just wasn't there. She died of some kind of complications from pneumonia. I was basically alone after that, if you didn't count the household help."

"My father worked a lot, was away a good deal." Allison tried not to sound judgmental, but it hurt. "I thought that if I studied very hard and followed him into the business he'd notice me, talk to me."

Angelo saw a small, sad smile curve her lips and knew he hated the man who had hurt her like this.

"He never talked, just said a few words here and there, usually critical. Finally I decided that enough was enough. I was going to strike out on my own. There was a firm in

Nevada that wanted to hire me and I said yes. Father was late for a meeting the day I picked to leave."

Her voice grew lower as she spoke, remembering. "I hadn't found the opportunity to tell him I was going. He'd been too busy to listen. His chauffeur was sick, so I volunteered to drive. I thought I'd get it over with quickly, you know, tell him and then that would be that."

She took a deep, steadying breath before she continued, but it didn't help. She hardly realized that he had taken her hand. "It was raining and suddenly there was this car careening into ours. It jumped the divider. I swerved, trying to get out of the way, but there was no place to go."

Her tears were falling now, and she didn't bother brushing them aside. "My father was in a coma for two weeks. When he finally regained consciousness, he was paralyzed." She looked at Angelo, her eyes bright with tears. "This strong, virile man who was used to dashing from place to place, leaving his mark on the world, was paralyzed. And I had done it to him." She could still hear his voice in her head, accusing her.

Angelo took his handkerchief from his pocket and wiped away her tears. How could she even think that? "Allison, it wasn't your fault."

But she shook her head adamantly. "If I hadn't been that overwrought, if I wasn't trying to find the right way to tell him that I was leaving, maybe even secretly hoping that he would ask me to stay, then maybe it wouldn't have happened." She had gone over it a hundred times in her head, always with the same tortured results. It was her doing.

He took her shoulders and shook her, trying to make her see reason. "That car still would have jumped the divider and run into you."

She passed a hand over her face. What was she doing, sitting here and crying? "If I had been alert, I would have seen it coming and avoided the accident."

He pocketed the handkerchief. "Maybe, maybe not. There are a thousand different things to take into account." He pressed the keys into her hand and then curled his hand around hers. She could feel the support, feel the empathy and strength. "Your father could have skipped the meeting or taken a cab. Allison, you can't control everything. Things do happen in this world through no fault of our own. You can't go on blaming yourself for the accident for the rest of your life."

She jabbed the key back into the ignition. "Maybe not. But I can make it up to him."

He knew what she meant by that. "How? By sacrificing yourself? I don't think he'd want that."

A mirthless smile lifted the corners of her mouth. "You don't know my father." He remembered everything. And forgave nothing.

He nodded, conceding the point. "Then introduce me."

She hadn't expected that. "What?"

"Introduce me," he repeated. "I'd like to meet him," He wanted to know what kind of a man held his daughter captive with guilt.

She shook her head firmly, releasing the hand brake. Then she started the engine and cruised on the shoulder, waiting for a spot to open up for her in the slow lane. "I don't think that's a good idea."

"Why not?" Angelo pressed. "Doesn't he take an interest in the people in your life?"

"He doesn't take an interest in me," she pointed out. "Why should he take an interest in the people in my life?" She stopped, realizing what she had said. "Besides, you're not in my life."

"Oh, yes, I am."

She didn't have to look. She heard the grin in his voice. "Look, Angelo, it's not fair to you or to me to start anything. I'm not free to feel anything. I have—"

"Obligations. Yes, I know. We just went all through that." He had an endless supply of patience, but she was making short work of it. He had never met anyone so mule-headed before. "How about your obligation to yourself?"

She shrugged, pulling into the lane and stepping on the gas. "I'm a general contractor. I have an engineering degree. I'm doing what I love doing."

She couldn't be an engineer twenty-four hours a day. "But when the lights go out—"

"I go to sleep," she said doggedly.

"Then I think it's time you woke up, Allison, woke up to the things that life has for you."

She slanted him a knowing look. They had come full circle. "Meaning you?"

"It's a start."

She was afraid, afraid of offering her affections, afraid of venturing forth on that shaky path. If her own father couldn't love her, why should anyone else?

But it was almost as if she had no choice. She had to take at least one step on the path, just one. She'd forever regret it if she didn't. "All right, after this visit with Miller, I'll have dinner with you." God, what had she gone and done? "But that's all. Dinner. Understood?"

"Understood. Now," he said, nodding at the wheel, "would you like me to take over, or are you up to driving?"

She felt embarrassed at being so weak before, of letting her emotions get the better of her. Of letting him see her like that. "I'm driving, aren't I?"

"Yes, you are."

She'd been too sharp. He didn't deserve that, not after he'd been so kind. Her voice softened. "Angelo?"

"Yes?"

"Thanks."

She didn't have to say any more. "No problem." He leaned back. "Okay, now let's go and kick some butt."

Allison laughed, shaking her head. He was one of a kind, all right.

The visit to Miller and Jones was a brief one. Harley Miller, Jr., was in a meeting when Allison and Angelo walked in, just as his secretary had claimed. The horrified woman tried to bar their way and was easily moved aside by Angelo, not physically but with charm. Allison was amazed. While he wasn't the best-looking man she had ever seen, there was something definitely appealing about him in an earthy sort of way.

And he was getting to her, more through his kindness than through the fact that he was sexy with a capital *S*.

After calming down Miller's secretary sufficiently enough so that she took her seat again behind her desk, Angelo turned toward Allison and gestured toward the door. "Commandos first," he said, winking.

Harley looked up, startled and annoyed at the interruption when they entered the room. "What are you doing here?" he demanded. "I'm in a meeting."

"This won't take long," Allison promised him sweetly, nudging aside the man who sat before Harley. She dropped the length of wire onto the highly polished conference table. The wire whispered along the surface. "Just explain this and we'll leave."

Harley looked at the wire and then at Allison. "This?" he repeated.

Allison saw the sweat beginning to bead on his upper lip. "It's below regulation, Harley." She pushed it closer to him. "If you bothered to look."

He took out his white handkerchief and mopped his brow, swiping the cloth along his lip, as well. "Um, it is?"

She hated deceit more than anything else, except, perhaps, the cold, appraising gaze in her father's eyes. "It is and you know it." Her voice lowered just a little, but there was no missing the authority behind it. "I don't want you

using this. I want the gauge we agreed on. If you don't re-
place this by tomorrow, not only do we cancel our order to
you, but by the time I'm through telling my story about how
you fraudulently altered the quality assurance report that
accompanied our order, you won't be able to sell enough
wiring to light up a birthday cake."

Miller looked from Allison's face to Angelo's and saw no
room for bargaining in either. "You'll have your wire."

It wasn't good enough for Angelo. He was well ac-
quainted with the type. Although his company was smaller,
he had been in the business, or on the fringes with his father, longer than Allison. "Tomorrow, nine sharp," he told
Harley evenly.

Harley bobbed his head. "Sharp," he echoed with a
nervous laugh.

"Nicely handled," Angelo murmured to Allison as they
walked out of the room.

Yes, she thought so, too. "I grew up watching John
Wayne westerns."

"I saw the resemblance." Angelo laughed, easily slipping his arm around her shoulders.

This time she didn't try to shrug it off. She realized that
she rather liked the comforting feeling of having it there.

Chapter Nine

As they returned to the parking lot in front of Miller's office, Angelo walked around to the driver's side of Allison's sedan. Their hands met over the handle. She looked at him quizzically, moving her hand away from his. "What are you doing?"

"Well, I thought that since you don't know where we're going and I do, I should drive." He put his hand out for the keys. "Unless, of course, you're possessive of your car. I could understand that. It is a beauty."

She had seen the car in an ad in her favorite magazine and had bought it on impulse. The only other thing she had ever done on impulse was take in Fate. Until now She handed Angelo the keys.

Angelo's eyes skimmed over the car as he got in behind the wheel. He thought of his brother. "Shad would love to take this out for a spin sometime if you didn't mind."

Allison barely had time to buckle up before they were zipping out of the lot. His driving, like his kiss, took her breath away. "I don't mind and I'm not possessive of my car. What I am possessive of is my person."

He glanced at her before he looked back at the road. "And well you should be. But there is something to be said for letting the right person share it with you."

She spread her hand on the glove compartment door to brace herself as the car just made it through a yellow light and swung into the car pool lane on the freeway entrance ramp. "You're going too fast."

She wasn't talking about the speed of the car and he knew it. "I can slow down." He eased back his foot and the car settled to just under the speed limit.

She realized that he had gotten on the ramp heading in the opposite direction from the mall. They were going south, not north. "Aren't we going back to the site?"

"No." He grinned. "Dinner, remember?"

There was that uncertainty again fluttering in her stomach. She pressed a hand to it. "Well, I might have said something that would have led you to believe—"

By now he was used to this. Two steps forward, one step back. But it was still progress. "I remember every golden word. You said you'd run off with me and have dinner on the beach at Waikiki."

She sat up. "I did not. I said I'd have dinner after this meeting with Miller was over." Her eyes met his and she realized she had been set up.

"Oh, so it does come back to you?"

"Just keep your eyes on the road, for heaven's sake." She laughed and shook her head. She liked him. He was brash and threatening in a way she couldn't begin to define, but she liked him. She couldn't go on denying that or hoping she was mistaken.

As the freeway lost a lane and threaded toward Newport Beach, she looked at her watch. There were still things she had left to do. And she had planned to stop by the office for some paperwork before she went home. She'd forgotten all about that. "This won't take too long, will it? Dinner, I mean." She felt a need to qualify her question, otherwise who knew what he'd come up with.

The freeway melted away as they emerged on a street. He took a turn on Harbor Boulevard. "I wasn't planning on going anywhere where the staff wears roller blades. Why?"

She looked at her watch again and realized she had done that three times already. Her nerves were ganging up on her. "It's just that I wanted to go over the blueprints for the dome one more time. There's something about it that bothers me." No, if she was being completely honest, there was something about being alone with him like this, without benefit of work or other people she could rely on, that bothered her, not the dome.

Angelo glanced at the digital clock on the dashboard. "It's after five."

"Yes, I know. So?" He could talk in riddles sometimes. "What does that have to do with it?"

He kept an eye out for the restaurant. Traffic was heavy at this time of the day. They were queueing up at each light. "Don't you punch out?"

Didn't he understand by now? "I'm not being paid by the hour."

He laughed. "Nobody could afford you if you were." The light changed and he switched lanes, working his way around two Volkswagens, then getting back into his lane. He made it through another light. "Hasn't anyone told you yet?"

"Told me what?"

He saw the tip of the pagoda on his right. So near and yet so far, he mused. "The eighties are over. We don't have to be superheroes or larger than life anymore. It's okay to kick back once in a while."

That again. Maybe he had stock in a mattress company. "I don't want to kick back, Marino. This is who and what I am."

He wasn't buying it. He hadn't before and he certainly wasn't now, not after that glimpse into her soul she had given him earlier. "Oh, no, there's a lot more to you than steel girders and retaining walls and rivets, Allison Conrad."

She wasn't going to debate him. She already knew that was useless. "This is a free country and you're entitled to your opinion, but since it is a free country, I don't have to listen." She turned up the radio, then raised her voice. "So if you'll just drop me off at the site."

Calmly he lowered the volume again. "Nope."

She couldn't believe this. "Nope?" she echoed incredulously.

"Nope."

For a moment she just stared at him. "Kidnapping is still a federal offense, you know."

"I hardly think that taking someone to see *Gone with the Wind* will stand up in court as an offense punishable by imprisonment." He worked his way into the right lane, preparing to turn at the next block. The restaurant he wanted was located in the center. "Now if I were going to take you to see *Heaven's Gate,*" he continued breezily, "there might be some—"

He had lost her in the very beginning. *"Gone with the Wind?"*

He nodded, bringing the car to a halt at a mini-mall. He parked several doors away from the restaurant. "It's playing not too far from here. Have you ever seen it?"

"Of course I—" She began to say yes automatically, but then stopped. What was the point of lying?

"Haven't."

He knew her answer before she said it. "You might be the only one in the United States who hasn't. Possibly the whole free world." He shook his head, trying to envision the type of life she had had. It had to have been austere to have shaped her philosophy about life. "What did you do while you were growing up?"

"I studied. Hard," she said proudly. "And I read a lot."

He pictured her, a small blond child in a large, fancy bedroom, sitting by herself. "Must have been lonely."

She didn't want his pity, or anything remotely resembling it. She had done just fine for herself. "I got along." He opened the door for her and she got out. "What happened to dinner?"

He grinned as he took her hand, linking his fingers one by one with hers. "I thought we'd stop for Chinese and take it with us."

Her hand felt secure in his, as if there wasn't anything that would ever hurt her. But, of course, that wasn't true. She knew better. Besides, there was still the fact that he was crazy. "Eat at the movies?"

He guided her toward the tiny storefront restaurant with the red door edged in gold paint. It gave a long, angular impression as the roof rose high into the sky. "Yeah, why not?"

The man just didn't think things through. "It's messy, for one."

As soon he opened the restaurant's door for her, the lush aroma seemed to surround her, reminding her that lunch had been three chocolate chip cookies. "The cartons are leakproof. Besides, if my hands are busy, you won't have to worry about me trying anything."

She walked to the tiny take-out counter. "I don't worry. I can handle myself."

He winked. "Yes, but it helps to have a chopstick in your hand."

With the food neatly packed in a brown sack, Angelo smuggled it into the theater by nonchalantly draping his jacket over it. Allison felt an uncontrollable urge to start giggling. This was almost like being a teenager, sneaking into a movie with forbidden fruit. The sign outside the cashier's booth strictly prohibited bringing in any food or drink.

She felt as if she was on a teeter-totter. Angelo made her feel like a kid, or how she supposed a kid might feel. A kid one minute, a woman the next. It was enough to confuse anyone.

They found a seat toward the front in the relatively empty theater. He leaned his head toward her as he handed her a napkin. "When I was very young, money was pretty tight. Movies were cheap then, but even so they were a rare treat. My mom used to take me to see the old classics whenever she could get a little put by. She'd make some fried chicken, pack a few cannolis and we'd sit in the last row, watching and eating."

Even in the dim light he saw the wistful look that passed over her face before she could shut it away. "What's the matter?"

She tried to concentrate on the beautiful music that flooded the theater as the credits began. "Nothing."

He didn't want to let it drop. He was making too much headway this afternoon to stop now. "No, c'mon, tell me. Was it something I said?"

"Yes." She managed a smile. "I just wondered what it would have been like, that's all, doing something like that with my mother."

He smiled at her. "A lot like this, except that you would have been shorter and had trouble seeing. Egg roll?"

She blinked back a tear that stubbornly materialized and accepted the bag he passed to her, grateful that he didn't try to probe too deeply. He was good for her. However long they were going to work together, she had a feeling that things would remain this way. There was something exceedingly comforting in that.

Allison had never made time for movies as an adolescent. Her life had been strictly regimented by a parade of unsmiling governesses handpicked by her father As she grew older, movies didn't capture her attention. Work and then her debt to her father had consumed her. She expected to be bored now, watching a fifty-year-old movie.

Instead, she was enchanted, caught up in the story and the strength that was Scarlett O'Hara. As she watched, engrossed, Allison identified with Scarlett, a woman making her way against tremendous odds, struggling and triumphing the only way she knew how.

It had been that way for her.

When the lights finally came up, Allison remained very quiet in her seat, the empty container of chicken lo mein neatly packed away in its bag. The chopsticks, Angelo noticed, were still clutched tightly in her hand.

The other people in the theater were all filing out, but she stayed where she was, deeply affected. Angelo had started to rise, then, seeing that she wasn't moving, dropped back into his seat. He took the bag from her, crushing it and depositing the whole thing into his own. "Pretty terrific, wasn't it?"

She turned her eyes slowly to his. It was then that he saw the tears. "You like that kind of thing?"

He wasn't certain what sort of response she was looking for from him. He could only be honest and hope. "Yeah, I like that kind of thing." Gently he eased the chopsticks from her.

She rose with a sigh. She was being silly. Why should a movie affect her so deeply? But it had. Scarlett had gained everything back and more, but had lost the only thing that counted. Love. "It doesn't have a happy ending."

Was that it? He felt relieved. Angelo took her hand and ushered her out of the lobby, dropping their empty bag into the trash can. "Sometimes things don't. Me, I like to rewrite my own endings."

She wiggled her fingers in his hand, not to get loose, but to absorb the feel of it. "And how would you rewrite this one?"

That was easy. He had already done it for himself the first time he had seen the movie. "Well, you see," he said, unlocking her door and then staying where he was, "Scarlett would spend some time at Tara, repenting and mending her ways. Just as she's about to go back and look for Rhett, there's a knock on the door." He looked and noted with pleasure that Allison appeared to hang on to his words. "She opens it and there he is—Rhett Butler." Angelo lapsed into a falsetto voice as he took the part of Scarlett. "'Oh, Rhett, you've come back to me.' And Rhett—" Angelo stopped as Allison's laughter swelled and echoed all around him. "Hey, no laughing here," he chided, trying his best to look offended. "This is serious stuff."

Allison lifted a hand. "Wait, wait, I promise not to—" And she laughed again. Then with great effort she sobered. He sounded absolutely ridiculous as Scarlett. And wonderfully endearing.

"Ready?" His voice was patient.

She nodded, biting the inside of her cheeks as she tried to keep a straight face. "Ready."

"Rhett sweeps her into his arms, like this." And Angelo did the same, despite the fact that they were standing in the middle of the parking lot, with people passing by all around them. "And he says..." Angelo drew a breath as he looked into Allison's eyes, changing his voice to that of a reasonably fair imitation of Clark Gable. "'Frankly, my dear, I *do* give a damn.'"

The words were meant to be Rhett's. All Angelo had intended to do on the outset was to give Allison her happy ending for the movie. But after the words were uttered, he realized that even though he was using someone else's voice, Angelo was telling Allison what was in his heart.

"You see," he told her in his natural voice, the cadence soft and low, "I like happy endings, too."

There was no choice. He had none from the moment he had looked into her eyes. Angelo lowered his mouth and kissed her.

She had always been a very private person, locking away everything, every feeling, every thought inside of her. What people didn't know they couldn't use against her. If she didn't let her father see she was hurt, he wouldn't know that he had hurt her. But now there was no holding back, no hiding place inside her to crawl away to. Angelo had made it crumble. She melted against him, despite the fact that they were standing in the center of a busy area and she would have never, in her wildest dreams, thought of letting someone kiss her in public, let alone this much public.

She let it happen now.

More than that, she wanted it to happen now.

She absorbed the taste of his mouth hungrily, her tongue gliding along his, first hesitantly, then eagerly. God, she wanted to be his. She wanted love so badly. But even as she craved it, she felt a hopelessness nudging along the perimeters of her mind.

Only the applause and the piercing whistles made her finally pull away. With an embarrassed laugh, hardly knowing what had come over her, she turned to their audience and gave a deep curtsy the way Scarlett might have.

Angelo hugged her to him, delighted. "Looks like we're not the only ones who like happy endings."

The euphoria of the moment slipped away and she cleared her throat nervously. "It's late. I really should be getting back."

He didn't want the day to end. "Nowhere else I can take you tonight?" he offered. "Ice-cream parlor? Shangri-la?"

"No." This time when she smiled there was almost something shy about it, he thought. He had made a major breakthrough today. His goal was in sight. "You've taken me to enough places for one day." She paused, looking up into his eyes. "Angelo?"

"Yes?"

"I had a nice time tonight."

"Yeah, me, too." He leaned a hip against the car as he played with a curl. He had a hard time keeping his hands away from her, he thought. "So you won't be pressing any kidnapping charges?"

"Not this time." She was getting caught up in his silliness. When she was with Angelo, she felt somehow lighter, freer than she had in a long time.

But the evening was over. She turned toward the driver's side. "I'll take you to your car." She looked up, surprised when he placed his hand over hers on the handle, stopping her. Was there somewhere else he intended to take her?

He found he could swim in those eyes of hers when she looked up at him like that. Swim in them and kiss her until his lips were numb. Maybe he'd get the opportunity sometime soon. "I'd rather take you home."

He wasn't making sense, but she had come to accept that aspect of him. "But your car is in the lot."

He shrugged. It was only a minor inconvenience. "I can call for a cab at your house. I'd like to see you home. That's the proper way to do things."

She thought of her father. He'd be home now. She didn't want things to be spoiled. It had been such a wonderful evening. "I wasn't aware that you were into the proper ways of doing things."

He grinned. "There are a lot of things about me you don't know." He bent his head and, ever so slightly, brushed a kiss alongside her neck. He heard her sigh. "Yet."

She struggled to focus. "Things that the mother of your children should know, right?"

He wanted to hug her, to hold her forever. He contented himself for now with just touching her cheek. "You're getting the hang of it."

She held his hand with both of her own, savoring the warm feeling. But she couldn't let herself believe in the rest of it. In a future that was any different from her past. "Angelo, that's a very interesting line—"

What would it take to make her finally believe? "It's not a line, Allison. It's a prediction. I had a great-aunt named Sophia who used to be able to tell your future by just looking into your eyes." He looked into hers meaningfully. "They say the gift skips a generation."

She took a step away, keeping the car to her back. "Sure you don't want me to take you to your car?" She worked her way to the passenger side.

"I'm sure."

She tossed him the keys over the roof, surrendering. Maybe he wouldn't ask to come in. "It seems like an awful lot of trouble to go to."

He got in. "I haven't got anything else to do tonight. Besides," he said, starting the car, "I'd like to meet your father."

The smile on her lips faded. So much for hoping that he would be content just to bring her to her doorstep and wait as she called a taxi. She frowned, thinking of a possible encounter. "I don't think—"

He knew what she was going to say and jumped in ahead of her. "As a fellow contractor if nothing else." They worked their way out of the parking lot, which was packed now with people out for the evening.

She didn't want the two meeting. She didn't want Angelo subjected to her father's cold scrutiny. "My father isn't very good with people, Angelo."

Finding an opening, Angelo pulled out. "I've already gathered that."

She felt her mouth grow dry at the prospect of the two men in the same room together. A strong, protective instinct rose up within her. It surprised her that she could have these kinds of feelings about Angelo. "It wouldn't be a good idea."

He heard the worry in her voice and wondered if she thought he'd bash her father. "Why don't you let me be the judge of that, Allison?"

"All right." She settled back, trying to face the situation calmly. "But don't say I didn't warn you."

He grinned as he took a route that would bring him to her door. He'd looked up her address after hearing her name. "Lady, you've been doing nothing but issuing me warnings since we first met and I haven't listened to one of them yet."

"No, that you haven't," she agreed. The statement didn't have nearly as much annoyance attached to it as she would have first thought it would.

As a matter of fact, it didn't have any at all.

For a large man Miles Conrad had small, piercing eyes. Blue and cold. He stared at Angelo through his thick glasses, seeming to burn away the lenses in his obvious displeasure at having his privacy interrupted by the man before him.

Pushing a button on the armrest, he turned the wheelchair to face Allison and block Angelo partially out. "You brought home a construction worker?"

Angelo got the distinct impression that Louis XIV would have said the same words in the exact same tone to his daughter, substituting the word *peasant* for *construction worker.*

She knew this was a mistake. She wished she had insisted that Angelo stay behind. But she was in the middle of this now, so she had to follow through. "Father, this is Angelo Marino. He and his partner are working on the other half of the mall extension with us."

Conrad totally ignored the hand Angelo extended in his direction. "Something going wrong, Marino?" he demanded.

"No." Angelo dropped his hand to his side. The man could freeze over a lake at ten paces in the middle of the summer, he thought, his heart hardening as he pictured Allison growing up here. "I just wanted to meet you."

The scowl grew deeper as Miles straightened in his chair. "Sizing up the competition?"

Angelo hooked his thumbs into his belt and looked completely at ease as far as Allison could tell. She didn't take note of the flicker of annoyance in his eyes. "I wasn't thinking of you as competition, sir."

Miles snorted and went back to reading his newspaper. "Well, at least you have brains enough to know your outfit isn't in our league."

"Yet."

Miles' head shot up as his fingers tightened on the paper "What was that?"

There was nothing to be gained by this. "Angelo." Allison placed her hand on his arm. There was an urgency in her touch. "I think you should go now. Edna's already called for the cab. It should be here any minute. Why don't we—?"

But Angelo wouldn't budge. He had always been easygoing, but that didn't mean he allowed himself to be pushed around or walked on. "I said yet," he repeated to Miles. "I think our work on this mall extension will be just the springboard our company needs to get into your league."

Miles threw down the newspaper. "How dare you? Just because she couldn't win the bid on her own—" he waved a disparaging hand at Allison "—and you're riding in on our coattails doesn't make you good, Marino."

If he had waved a red flag in front of a bull, the reaction couldn't have been more instantaneous. Angelo had to fight back an angry oath. The old fool. In one sentence he had managed to alienate and insult Marino and McClellan and Allison. What hell she must have gone through being brought up in this house.

Angelo managed to keep his voice level. "Marino and McClellan don't ride in on anyone's coattails, Mr. Conrad.

Our work speaks for itself." He turned toward Allison. "I'll see you tomorrow, Allison."

His tone gave no indication that he wanted her to follow him. She watched him leave, feeling an overwhelming wave of anger and helplessness wash over her.

Her father's voice brought her back. "What do you mean, bringing a man like that into my house?"

God, how she hated the way he tore people apart. "It's my house, too, Father. And you don't know a single thing about 'a man like that.'"

"You'll keep a civil tongue in your head when addressing me," Miles roared at her.

Fury left her cold. "If you'll excuse me, Father, I suddenly don't feel like being very civil tonight." She spun on her heel, walking out of the room as quickly as she could, ignoring the words her father shouted after her.

Chapter Ten

Angelo sat at his kitchen table, nursing a cup of black coffee that had long since cooled. He slowly turned pages of the Sunday newspaper he didn't really see.

He couldn't get Friday night out of his mind, not any of it.

He had always been able to size up people and situations quickly, as well as fairly accurately. It was a trait he and Shad shared. Just as Angelo had decided that beneath Allison's rigid exterior there existed a warm, giving woman he wanted to make a permanent part of his life, Angelo realized that beneath the rigid exterior of Miles Conrad there existed nothing more than a rigid interior.

It was a person's eyes that gave away secrets better than any telltale movements or phrases. Miles's eyes were cold, stone-cold, without a flicker of anything human within them.

Finally tasting his coffee, Angelo frowned and rose to pour it out. He poured himself another. Black liquid sloshed into his mug as he stared at the coffeemaker's hypnotic red light and wondered what would have made a woman marry someone like that. What could have prompted Allison's mother to waste herself on a man like Conrad?

Angelo set the pot back on the hot plate and sat down again. Speculation aside, for whatever reason, the woman had married Conrad. Together they had produced a beautiful creature who couldn't be allowed to view her life in terms of blueprints and endless quests to please a father who would never be pleased.

Angelo took a sip and felt the hot liquid spread through his system. He needed a way to melt down Allison's defenses permanently.

He decided to bring in the big guns. He was going to invite her to Sunday dinner at his mother's house. If being around Mrs. Marino and the others didn't make Allison yearn for a life beyond concrete and steel girders, then he sorely missed his guess about the inner woman. And he sincerely doubted that he did.

He didn't have to call his mother to warn her that he was bringing someone. She had been hounding him relentlessly to do just that for what seemed like years. What he did need to do, however, was get hold of Allison.

Easier said than done.

When he dialed her number, he was surprised that her father answered. Someone like Conrad didn't seem the type to answer his own phone. Angelo had hoped to talk to the Conrad housekeeper, if not Allison herself. Talking to Miles made things difficult.

"Sonny is not here," the man informed him tersely after Angelo identified himself.

"Do you know where she is?" Angelo asked quickly, knowing Conrad would hang up if he wasn't fast enough. "I'd like to invite her over for Sunday dinner."

"She takes Sunday dinners with me." The connection was abruptly broken before Angelo had the chance to ask anything further.

"Nice talking to you, too," Angelo muttered as he replaced the receiver. He stared at it for a moment, debating his options. Angelo always had options. To think otherwise was to admit defeat, and that was something totally foreign to him. Especially when the stakes were as high as this.

On the outside chance that Allison was actually at home and Miles was just being perverse, Angelo drove over to the Conrad house. When he knocked, to his relief the housekeeper answered the door. When he first met her the other evening, he had expected to see an austere, solemn woman. It would have been in keeping with the temperament within the walls of this structure. Nothing could have made him call it a home. But Edna Keller was a middle-aged woman with sparkling blue eyes and a warm personality.

Edna, Allison had confided, was the only one with enough stamina to stick it out whenever Miles had one of his explosions.

His mind on Allison, Angelo found he suddenly couldn't remember the older woman's name. "Edna, isn't it?" Angelo asked, fumbling through his memory.

She bobbed her head. Gray bangs shifted into her eyes. "It has been for the past sixty-eight years." She pushed the bangs aside as she looked at him. "What can I do for you, Mr. Marino?"

The woman was as warm as Conrad was cold. "Would you know if Allison is in?"

"No." She peered over her shoulder to see if they were still alone. Her employer was nowhere to be seen. Edna lowered her voice, just in case. "This is Sunday. If she doesn't go to the construction site, Sonny goes to the health spa to work out. She usually stays there from about ten to one."

The house was definitely large enough to have an indoor gym if she had wanted one. He guessed that Allison enjoyed not being at home as much as she enjoyed exercising.

He looked at Edna hopefully. "Could you be more specific? Which health spa?"

The fine lines of Edna's face softened as she smiled. The twinkle was hard to miss. "Are you sweet on her, Mr. Marino?"

A matchmaker, like his mother, he thought, amused. That was okay. He could use all the help he could get. "Angelo," he corrected. "And, yes."

She nodded, pleased. "About time someone like you showed up in her life." Edna wrote down the address of the spa for him on a scrap of paper.

The receptionist at Squire's Health Spa took a long, hard look at Angelo's muscular torso and decided the man was obviously serious about scouting out the facilities for a possible membership. Calling over an assistant to man the phone, even though it was generally slow on Sundays, the young woman volunteered to show Angelo the layout personally.

But as they passed the first doorway, he saw Allison on the exercise cycle. There was no one else in the room. Angelo quietly informed the chattering woman at his side that he wanted to look around on his own. She left him reluctantly.

For a moment Angelo stood in the doorway, simply watching her. Allison was apparently oblivious to her surroundings. She showed the same single-minded focus that he had observed over the weeks at the construction site. Dedication. She had it written all over her. Complete dedication to anything she turned her attention to.

He was going to enjoy shifting that dedication to himself.

Allison wore simple gray shorts with an elastic band and a tank top that adhered to her sleek, wet body. It riveted his attention. A frayed pink sweatband absorbed the perspiration beneath her bangs. One would have never known that she could have afforded the most expensive designer clothing. She seemed happiest in simplicity, he thought. It was a good sign.

She increased her speed, leaning forward over the handle bars, her legs pumping quickly. Perspiration glistened on her body. To look at her made his mouth water. She was poetry in motion.

She had earphones on, attached to a tape recorder at her waist. He wondered if she was listening to music or something that was work-related. It would be like her. He glanced at his watch. It was getting late. If he was going to make dinner, he was going to have to do a lot of convincing in a short amount of time.

Allison didn't notice him until he stood directly in front of her bicycle. The Tara theme filled her head. She had purchased the *Gone with the Wind* soundtrack on her way home Saturday. Listening to it reminded her of Angelo and Friday night. She had conjured him up so vividly in her mind that when he walked in front of her, her foot slipped off the pedal and she almost fell to the side.

Catching her breath, she pulled the earphones down around her neck and blinked, staring at him. He was real. "What are you doing here?"

He placed his hands on the handlebars and leaned forward until his face was inches from hers. Inches that tantalized them both. "Watching you push yourself. You really don't know how to take things easy, do you?"

She got off the bicycle and grabbed a towel from a rack, wiping her forehead. "How did you find me?" Shutting off the tape, she placed the recorder on a nearby bench and then sank down next to it.

He joined her. "Edna told me."

"Edna?" she repeated in surprise.

"Your housekeeper."

"I know who Edna is. When did you talk to her?"

"This morning. I came to the house." When she stared at him in silence, he asked, "What are you doing here?"

She gestured toward the equipment around her. She'd been here for almost two hours. "Exercising." What was he doing, coming over to her house? Hadn't one run-in with her father been enough?

"Why here? You could build an elaborate gym at home."

She shrugged. He was prodding her. "I like it here. Away from home," she added, knowing that was what he was after.

He placed his hand on her arm. The effect was incredibly comforting. She wondered if he knew. "Why don't you move out?"

She shrugged again, looking away. It was hard talking to those eyes. They seemed to see everything. "I can't."

"Why?"

It was a small word. It demanded so much. "He needs me."

If ever a human being had made a religion out of not needing any human contact, it was Miles Conrad. "He doesn't need anything but a heart transplant."

She wished he'd stop making her examine this hurt. She didn't want to think about it. "I promised him I'd stay with the business."

She was shackled and he wanted her to break free. Not for him, for herself. But no one could do it for her. He could only point things out. "I think he's perfectly capable of running everything."

She got up and walked onto the treadmill. Switching it on, she began keeping pace. "I owe him."

He moved in front of her so that she couldn't look away. "You owe him a degree of filial love. Respect. Not your life, Allison."

She couldn't exercise like this, not with him confronting her. With an angry huff she switched off the machine again. "Did you come looking for me to deliver a lecture?"

He was being impatient and he knew it. No one else in his family was hot-blooded. And neither was he. Generally. He supposed it was a recessive gene and right now it felt as if he had gotten everyone else's share. "No, I came to invite you to dinner."

Her mouth curved. "More Chinese food at the front of the theater?"

"Actually, that doesn't sound like a bad idea, but I was thinking more in terms of a meal at my mother's." He saw the guarded look that rose into her eyes. He was losing her. "It's a ritual with her. She has the family over every Sunday. Anyone who doesn't show up had better have an excuse verified by the Pope or they risk excommunication."

Allison slung the towel back around her shoulders. "I'm not part of the family."

Gently he tugged her hair out from under the towel. His hands remained on her shoulders. "It wouldn't hurt to meet them, would it?"

She couldn't be anything but honest with him. "I don't know."

He really wanted her to meet everyone. And them her. "Hey, I wasn't wrong about seeing *Gone with the Wind*, was I? You liked it, didn't you?" Gently he started massaging her shoulders. Despite the exercise routine she had just gone through, he could feel knots there.

She began to relax. It was strange how his touch could both excite her and bring her languid contentment at the same time. "Yes, but—" The protest was begun without much enthusiasm.

"You'll like Ma. Think of it as bringing joy to an old woman's heart."

She turned to look up at his face. "How will seeing me do that?"

He grinned, thinking of his mother. With Shad and Dottie married her full attention was now on him. Specifically

on finding him a wife. "Seeing the empty chair next to mine
filled will do that."

She bit her lower lip, hesitating. Afraid. "I don't
know—"

"I do."

Even as Allison stood next to Angelo at the front door of
a small two-story house, dressed in the simple skirt and
blouse she had brought with her to the spa, she was still
wondering how he had managed to get her there. She had no
desire to meet his family, to have a brief glimpse into a place,
a life where she could never enter. Years ago, after the accident, she had come to terms with her life-style, with what
the future would hold for her. Why did he have to torture
her with something she knew she could never allow to happen? There was no point to it.

She was just about to inform him that she had changed
her mind about having dinner when the front door opened.
A woman with salt-and-pepper hair and eyes the same color
as Angelo's stood before her. Allison saw the resemblance
immediately. It was in the smile.

Bridgette Marino was two inches shorter than Allison and
about twenty pounds heavier. When she opened the door,
Allison expected the woman to scrutinize her closely. She
had only her own father to go by.

Bridgette enveloped Allison in a soft, warm hug, then
held her at arm's length to study her face. Mrs. Marino
knew without being told who this woman was. After listening to Angelo talk, she had been expecting her, if not this
Sunday, then the next. It was only a matter of time.

Allison was a little thin for Bridgette's taste, but a suc-
cession of Sunday dinners would remedy that in time. "Ah,
you are finally here." She gave Angelo a satisfied look.
"Come in, come in." She turned, leading the way into her
living room.

Allison couldn't believe it. "You told your mother about me?"

He didn't know if that pleased her or not. He only saw wonder in her eyes. Angelo linked his fingers with hers as he followed his mother. "I might have said a word here, a word there. Ma likes to embellish as she goes along. We humor her."

On the construction site she felt confident. She knew what she was about. At a board meeting her facts were straight, her figures all double-checked for accuracy. She could speak with assuredness. She didn't frequent cocktail parties because she had no control there. She had less here.

For the first time in her life Allison wanted to turn and flee.

Angelo sensed the tension, the uncertainty coursing through her. He squeezed her hand. "Come meet everyone," he coaxed.

She did her best to look brave.

The living room, its walls lined with framed photographs of all sizes, some faded, some not, seemed crammed as people flowed in from two sides, surrounding her. She felt only slightly heartened when she saw a familiar face and nodded at Shad.

Angelo placed an arm around her shoulders. "You already know Shad. That's J.T., his wife."

Allison looked at a tall, regal woman at Shad's side. When she smiled at Allison, there was a comforting warmth that emanated from her. Allison thought she saw a kinship there.

Angelo pulled down the brim of a California Angel's cap over a tall blond boy's eyes. "This handsome guy is their son, Frankie." He bent down and scooped up a sunny-looking little girl who had a pink band falling over one eye instead of on her head. She couldn't have been more than a year old. "The little person drooling on your shoes is their daughter, Bridgette."

After kissing the tiny golden head, he passed the baby to Shad. Turning, he nodded at the woman on Allison's right. "This peaked-looking creature is my sister Dottie. She isn't normally green, but she's pregnant right now." He grinned at his sister. He thought that at this moment he was probably more excited about her pregnancy than Dottie was. He knew that he couldn't wait to hold the tiny new person in his arms. The only thing that gave Angelo more pleasure than the children in his extended family was anticipating a time when he would have children of his own to play with and love. Allison's children.

Suddenly Allison found her hand enveloped in a hearty grip by the blonde Angelo was introducing. The woman might be feeling queasy, but there was nothing wrong with her strength, Allison noted.

"Hi!" Dottie's exuberance was hard to resist. "It's so great to meet you."

Allison could almost believe that the woman meant what she said. She looked so sincere. But why would she be happy to meet her? It was something Allison couldn't understand.

Angelo continued the introductions. "The guy in the expensive suit who looks like he thinks he invented fatherhood is her husband, Shea." He slipped an arm around a slim young teenager, hugging her to him. "This is their daughter, Alex, and you've already met Ma." He stood back, finished. "That's all of us." So far, he added silently.

Pride was brimming over in his voice. A twinge of envy seized Allison. How wonderful to feel proud of your family, to want to introduce them to someone and say: "These are my people." She was a descendant of a prestigious line, the daughter of a man who had his name stamped on some of the finest structures in the county, not to mention a number that were spread throughout the country. She would have traded it all in the blink of an eye for what Angelo had.

For what Angelo felt. There was love here. Pride born of love. Not pride evolving from an accident of birth.

She shook hands all around and fixed a smile on her face, feeling unaccountably nervous, as if she didn't belong here amid all this love and would be found out at any moment. The dark-haired woman Angelo had introduced as J.T. took advantage of the momentary lull to place her hand on Allison's arm and lead her toward the photo gallery on one wall.

Allison waited for a tour of the various faces depicted there. She had to admit, looking at the gallery, that the sight of the small, happy faces had her yearning, for the first time, for a child of her own. She brushed aside the thought quickly. That kind of thinking was absurd. She'd probably make an awful mother. She knew absolutely nothing about the way a mother should behave. For that matter Angelo would probably make a better mother than she would. He apparently had the hang of it.

"This is just an excuse," J.T. murmured, gesturing at the photographs. "I thought you might need a breather right about now."

A rueful smile flitted over Allison's lips. She was usually better than that at hiding her thoughts. "Is it that obvious?"

J.T. nodded. There was sympathy in her eyes. "You had the same look that I imagine I had when Shad brought me over for Sunday dinner." She leaned closer and whispered, "Scared."

"I'm not scared," Allison said. J.T. arched a skeptical eyebrow. Allison relented a little. "They're just a little overwhelming, that's all."

J.T. laughed. There was a warm lilt in her voice. "That they are. It isn't often a person runs into a wall of love like this." She paused for a moment before confiding in Allison, "I never had it."

Allison looked at J.T., surprised that the woman would admit something so personal to a virtual stranger.

J.T. looked at Allison understandingly. "I held that much love highly suspect. But it's genuine. Make no mistake about it. They really want to like you." J.T. looked into Allison's eyes, reassuring her. "We all do."

It made no sense to her. It wasn't logical. "Why?"

"Because Angelo singled you out and we all love Angelo. He's a very warm and loving man. You should see him with the children." J.T. looked over toward the next room, where Frankie and Alex were plying him with questions about something. "Angelo always seems to make time for them no matter what." She turned back to Allison. "That's a very rare trait in a man."

Allison thought of her own father. She couldn't remember spending a single evening with him as a child. There were no stories, no games, no outings. She had no idea that fathers even did that sort of thing until she was in her teens. "Yes, I know."

"You're making her frown," Dottie said to J.T. playfully, coming up behind Allison. "Angelo wouldn't like that."

Allison flushed. "I'm sorry. I was just thinking about something."

Dottie cocked her head and studied her for a moment. "Work?"

It was easier to lie than go into the truth. The truth was far too painful to share, even with people who seemed eager to take on her burdens. "Yes."

Dottie nodded knowingly. "J.T. had the same problem until Shad turned her around."

"There's nothing wrong with being involved in work," J.T. clarified for Allison. "But not when it consumes your life."

"No," Dottie agreed, linking her arm casually through Allison's and leading her back into the center of the room. Into the center of activity. "Not when it makes you miss the best part of life."

"You work?" Allison hoped she didn't sound as surprised to them as she did to her own ears. She hadn't meant it to come out like that. To her relief neither woman appeared to take offense.

"J.T.'s an accountant with her own firm," Dottie told her. "And I'm a child psychologist."

As soon as she declared her profession, Allison involuntarily tensed. "Don't worry. I don't work on Sunday," Dottie said with a wink.

Allison returned the smile, trying desperately to relax. This was a completely unfamiliar situation to her and she wasn't certain how to act. Relaxing wasn't her normal state, not around people at any rate. But then she thought of Angelo and the movie they had gone to see. Maybe she could learn.

Bridgette Marino joined the cluster of women. She placed one hand on Allison's shoulder. "Can you peel?"

Allison blinked, certain she hadn't heard the question correctly. "Excuse me?"

"Potatoes," Bridgette enunciated slowly. "Can you peel them?"

"Well, yes, I can," Allison answered haltingly. No one had ever asked her anything like that. She was used to fielding engineering questions, even at the few parties her work necessitated that she attend. Culinary abilities had never come up.

She didn't do her best work in the kitchen. Edna always insisted on making all the meals. But there had been occasions, when she lived by herself, that she had passed over the frozen dinners in her freezer and attempted meals made from scratch.

Her success rate was another story, of course.

"Good." Bridgette nodded. She wanted to make sure Angelo wouldn't starve, marrying this girl. She had taught him how to cook, just as she had taught the others, but it would be comforting to know that his wife was capable of preparing something, as well. Besides, there were things to be learned in a quiet kitchen that couldn't be discovered in the middle of a noisy crowd. "Come, I need help."

So saying, Bridgette Marino took possession of the woman she already knew would be the future Mrs. Angelo Marino and led her off to the kitchen.

Allison looked toward Angelo for help, but there was a twelve-month-old on his back. Angelo was on all fours and whinnying. The sight filled her with inexplicable tenderness. Seeing him like that, Allison could almost picture Angelo with their own child—

Allison blotted out the thought, rejecting it as impossible. She was getting too caught up in all this. This kind of life wasn't meant for her. She knew exactly what her future held, and it didn't include a husband or children.

Still, she let herself be led away.

Chapter Eleven

Bridgette Marino looked at the young woman sitting at her kitchen table, peeling potatoes. The skins that lay in a heap in front of her were a bit too thick for Bridgette's liking, but that was neither here nor there. The chore was merely an excuse to be alone with Allison. She wanted no distractions when she talked to the woman her son had chosen. While Bridgette loved the three children she had raised under her roof equally, there was still a special bond between her and Angelo, the only child of her flesh. She wanted to see him happy. She wanted to be assured that this young woman with the delicate cheekbones and determined chin could make him happy.

She dropped another potato into the bowl of water. "So you work with Angelo?"

The soft voice, coming unexpectedly, nearly made Allison slice her finger. She tightened her grip on the knife and offered a nervous smile. "No, that is, we're both working on the mall extension, but I represent a different company. Conrad and Son."

Bridgette rose and cleared away the potato peels. Her heap was twice as big as Allison's. Not very handy in the kitchen, but not inept, either. And willing. That counted for a lot.

"Yes, Angelo told me. You're the 'Son.'" She pushed several potatoes toward Allison, intent on keeping the woman with her a little longer. "I just need a few more." She picked up the bowl of small, peeled potatoes and deposited the lot into the large pot of boiling water. "I was not sure if he would bring you this time."

Allison looked up, surprised. "This time?"

Bridgette nodded. "I have been telling Angelo to bring you to dinner ever since Shad told me about you."

Allison couldn't help feeling awkward and stupid, parroting everything that the older woman said. It just seemed to happen. "Shad told you about me?" What could he have said?

Bridgette moved around the kitchen, tasting, stirring, adding a pinch of something here, a dash there, and creating magical smells that made Allison's mouth water. "He told me about the way Angelo looked at this certain girl and I asked him for the girl's name." She turned to look at Allison. There was a warm smile in her eyes. "Shad told me yours."

Allison couldn't let this sweet woman get the wrong impression. It wouldn't be fair. "Mrs. Marino, I'm not sure what anyone has told you, but I'm completely dedicated to my father's company—"

The sound of a lid clattering on top of a pot cut Allison off. "And your father, he approves?"

Approves wasn't the word. Allison doubted if he approved of anything that concerned her. "He expects it."

"Ah." Understanding etched itself into the lines around Bridgette's mouth. "Does he expect you to be married to your work as well?"

Allison continued peeling, studying the potato in her hand. "In a way, I suppose."

"It is a lonely life. My husband, he started the company Angelo and Shad run now. Then he only worked in tile. Bathrooms, small things." She gestured to the kitchen floor and its neatly laid blue tile with tiny white flowers. "They had the vision." She nodded toward the living room. "But it never became so big that it gobbled up either one of them."

She took the last potato from Allison's hand and smiled into the eyes of a troubled young woman as their hands touched. "Work is a very good thing, my dear. As long as it does not become the only thing. You have to control it, not it you." She put the last potato into the pot. "There, the potatoes are all cooking. Tell Angelo you have been a big help to me." She waved both hands at Allison, indicating that she was dismissed.

Allison turned and walked out of the kitchen, directly into Angelo's arms. He grinned as he tightened them around her. "Hi." He brushed a kiss against her temple. "I was just looking for you."

She couldn't believe how comforting that felt. How natural. "Your mother had me in the kitchen peeling potatoes." A contented smile slipped across her face. She knew that all this was just an afternoon in a life that was light-years away from her own, but while she was here she could pretend that this was part of her life and not just an aberration.

Angelo looked over her head toward the kitchen. A swinging door separated the two rooms. "Really?"

The collar of his shirt was slightly crooked, probably because of his role as a horse for little Bridgette's amusement. Allison straightened it with the tips of her fingers. It was a simple thing to do, but it added to the glow she felt inside. "Why do you look so surprised?"

"Ma doesn't like anyone in her kitchen when she's working. She claims they just mess her up. She's given you her stamp of approval." It meant a lot, having his family take her in like this. It wouldn't have changed his feelings for Allison if they hadn't, but it did make things better.

"She's a nice lady." Maybe her own mother would have been like that had she lived.

"We think so."

It was an illogical thing to believe, but Allison found herself fitting in. She had always felt awkward being around displays of affection. Yet somehow it seemed as if there was a niche with her name on it in the Marino household. She had absolutely no idea how it had evolved in the space of a few hours. She only knew that she felt as if she belonged and that she liked it. More than she would have ever imagined. It was like growing. You weren't aware of it until one day you measured yourself and found that you were taller, bigger, without having noticed that it was happening at all. At the outset, when she entered holding Angelo's hand, she had felt like odd woman out. But by evening's end she was listening to the talk around the table and laughing. And joining in. It felt wonderfully normal.

She was one of them. At least for tonight.

Angelo watched her blossom and knew that he had made the right move by bringing her here. There was something about his mother that created almost a magic circle of love. It wasn't anything she said; it was just the way she was. He remembered the way Shad and Dottie had been when they first arrived, frightened, withdrawn, uncommunicative. Shad had been particularly hostile, having borne the brunt of constant rejection. Just by being in the house, by associating with Salvator and Bridgette Marino, the children had been pulled out of themselves, their potential fully realized until they developed into the fulfilled individuals they were now.

Angelo was certain that the magic of his mother's kindness would help Allison, as well. He couldn't do it on his own. And he was never ashamed of needing help. The future of his unborn children depended on it.

"So," Angelo said, smiling at her as he brought Allison to her doorstep, "you've survived the encounter."

He was teasing her. This time it pleased rather than annoyed her. She was grateful to him. Grateful for being allowed to spend an afternoon amid such mutual affection, such unspoken, unqualified love. It made her feel a little better about the world at large and about herself, as well. Things couldn't be totally bad if people like Angelo's family existed in the world.

She had an urge to touch his face, but that wasn't like her. She linked her fingers awkwardly. "I had a very nice afternoon. Thank you."

Patiently he wedged his hand between hers until he could hold one. "It's me who should be thanking you. For once Ma wasn't asking me why I was alone."

She laughed, thinking of the few minutes she had spent alone in the kitchen with Bridgette. "I think she was making plans for a wedding."

A breeze lifted. Her hair moved into her face. He brushed it aside tenderly. She would be his eventually, but not soon enough to suit him. "Well, that would make two of us."

She moved aside. There was no point in going over this. "Angelo, I can't."

He placed his hands on her shoulders and made her look at him. "It's not because you don't care."

"No," she admitted, surprised at her own frankness. She believed in honesty, but most of all she was a private person. This afternoon had opened a lot of doors. She had seen what it was like beyond her little world. She didn't want to be that private anymore. And yet she couldn't help it. Years of training were hard to break. "It's not because I don't care. But I told you once, I'm not free."

He wasn't going to accept that. And someday neither would she. "You're as free as you let yourself be, Allison." He placed a finger to her lips when she began to protest. "You're not your father's keeper. The most any child owes their parent is to be a good person. And to be happy."

She frowned and sighed. Suddenly she was sharing a lot more with him than she had ever dreamed she would with anyone. "He doesn't care if I'm happy. He only cares if I'm good."

Angelo took her into his arms. "Oh, you're good. You're very, very good." He nipped her lower lip, running his tongue over it, and she moaned, knowing what was to follow, wanting to sink into that warm, churning sea that he always led her to.

She had been waiting for this all afternoon.

Her eyes fluttered shut as the warmth, the excitement, came to her. In waves. In huge, wonderful, comforting, arousing waves. She felt safe. She felt exhilarated.

And above all she felt loved.

She knew it was just a small haven and that soon she'd have to leave port, but for now, just for now, she clung to it. She raised her mouth hungrily to his, greedily taking what he so freely gave her. It was as if she couldn't get enough. And she couldn't. She wouldn't ever have enough, no matter how much she tried to store it up.

The pretenses were gone. She was needy and she needed him, needed this. No one had ever offered her love before. Sex, yes. There had been that boy in college. Her first romance. A meaningless encounter fueled by her self-doubts, her need to have someone want her. It hadn't been her he had wanted. It had just been the satisfaction of having her. She had withdrawn from that experience just as she had from everything else, drawing a curtain around herself and struggling to survive. To protect her hurt feelings at being rejected.

She raised herself on her toes, desperate to drink, to satiate herself. Perhaps this afternoon had made her more vulnerable. Maybe being in the presence of so much love had made her yearn for just a little of her own. And Angelo kept telling her that he had it to offer.

For now she could pretend that he did.

"My God," she breathed, her voice raspy as she continued to cling to him, "I'm standing in front of my house, necking like a teenager." Color rose to her cheeks, but it was from exhilaration, not embarrassment.

He laughed, framing her face. "No teenager I ever knew could hold a candle to you."

Oh, she wanted to believe. So badly, she wanted to believe. "You keep saying all these nice things—"

He heard the denial coming and wouldn't let it. "I keep meaning all these nice things," he corrected. "You bring them out of me." He tucked a strand of hair behind her ear. Unable to resist, he dropped another kiss onto her lips, then slowly ran his tongue along his own lips, savoring the flavor. He had been right all along. She tasted like ripe strawberries. He had always loved strawberries. "Have lunch with me tomorrow."

Tomorrow. A whole different world waited out there tomorrow. "Tomorrow we go back to work."

Now that he had seen her like this, relaxed, laughing, he wasn't going to let her retreat again. "It's not exactly like going back to undercover work. There aren't any secret identities involved." He ran his hands slowly up and down her arms. "Lady engineers are allowed to fall in love."

"I didn't say I was in love." But just the simplest touch of his hand created a fire in her.

"Okay." They both knew that she was lying. And she knew that he knew. " 'In like' then."

She shook her head. Laughter bubbled up. "You don't give up, do you?"

"Never." Angelo pulled her close to him again, enjoying the way she fitted against him. "People who give up don't win."

She searched his eyes, wondering why he had singled her out like this, if even for a moment. Was it the thrill of the hunt? "I didn't think winning was important to you."

"Some things—" he lowered his mouth to hers again "—are very important to me."

She pulled away after a moment, afraid to let herself drift again. She wanted to make love with him, but the consequences were too great. She wouldn't be able to bear up to the rejection once it was over. Some things were best left unknown. "You start that again and we might be out here all night."

"There are worse fates." He rested his forehead against hers.

She was tempted. But they both needed their sleep. And she needed time to think. "We have a mall extension to bring in under budget and on time."

He sighed. "The penalty clause."

"It's a whopper."

"You said the magic word, Cinderella." He released her, taking a step back. "But someday you won't have that to hide behind."

And then, she thought sadly as she watched him walk to his car, you'll be gone.

But for now she wasn't going to think of that. She couldn't bear to.

With the two wings completed the two companies joined forces to construct the third and final one. The apex of the structure was the emerald dome that joined all three new wings and brought them together with the rest of the existing mall. The penalty clauses had fallen away one by one and the last one faded as they found themselves a week ahead of schedule.

But as speed increased, Angelo's headway with Allison slipped out of first gear. She was avoiding him, and although he had strong suspicions as to why, he wasn't about to let her fear or her commitments drive a wedge between them.

He found her in a small corner of the last wing, poring over yet another blueprint. She was chewing on a pencil and scowling. He wondered what she would do if he simply swept her up into his arms and kissed her the way he wanted to. Or better yet, took a page out of Rhett Butler's book and carried her up some staircase to make wild, passionate love with her.

It was tempting.

"Ma keeps asking when you're coming back."

She started, then took a breath to calm down. She had been so wound up in her work that she hadn't heard anything, much less his approach. "I've been busy with the modifications on the design for the dome." She laid the pencil down and rolled up the blueprint. "Grayson is an 'artiste' and very temperamental. Talking him into changes has been a bear." She snapped two rubber bands around the blueprint to hold it together. Carefully she avoided his eyes. "I haven't even had time to go to the health spa."

But Angelo shook his head. He divested her of the blueprint, tossing it aside. It would all be ironed out in the end. "Ma doesn't accept 'busy.' She's instructed me to come by your house and take you by force if necessary."

Allison laughed at the image that created. It jibed with the caveman identity she had once assigned him. She'd been horribly wrong. No "caveman" could have ever been as kind and understanding as Angelo. "I'll come this Sunday. Grayson has finally relented on the design. Otherwise that dome of his just wouldn't work."

Someone tapped her on the shoulder. Joseph was standing behind her, his face even paler than normal.

"What's the matter, Joseph? Didn't the crystal arrive yet?"

He nodded. "The last shipment just came, Sonny. And so did your father."

Her eyes widened. This was totally unlike her father. She looked at Joseph for some explanation, but he had none. "Father didn't tell me he was coming to the site. He doesn't generally make an appearance until after the project is completed." She felt apprehension begin to build. She braced herself for what she was coming. What always came.

Angelo saw her expression change. She looked like a cavalry officer waiting for the first wave of Indians to attack the wagon train. "Trouble?" He placed a protective hand on her arm.

She rubbed her thumb over her forefinger as she drew herself up. "Nothing I can't handle." She didn't want him here when her father came. It would only make things worse. She just knew it. "Why don't you go about your business and—"

He wasn't about to leave her alone now. She'd been alone too long as it was. "You are my business."

"Angelo, please."

He didn't like refusing her anything, but this time he had to follow his own better instincts. He put it in terms she could relate to. "You weren't the only one who grew up on westerns. I like to ride shotgun."

There was no more time for arguing. Out of the corner of her eye Allison saw her father approaching, two executives from the company on either side of his wheelchair like a solemn vanguard. She was reduced to the age of twelve again, hating it, hating the inadequate feeling that rose at the mere hint of his scrutiny.

Damn, why did she feel this way? The work was good and she was proud of it, proud of her crew and what they had accomplished. But she knew it wouldn't be good enough in her father's eyes. It never was.

"Sonny." He nodded curtly at his daughter, stopping his wheelchair before her. He completely ignored Angelo. Allison felt her temper flaring. It was typical of his small-minded behavior. He didn't care for Angelo, so for him Angelo didn't exist.

She took a step closer to Angelo. "You didn't tell me you were coming, Father."

The cold blue eyes narrowed. "Since when do I have to clear coming to my own work site with you?"

She wasn't going to let him browbeat her. Not this time. "I just thought you'd give me fair warning." But then *fair* had never been a word that had meant much to her father. Only getting his way did.

"Why?" He turned the chair in a wide arch, looking around at the work. "What is it you want to hide?"

"Nothing." He really was a petty, suspicious man. She was dropping off the rose-colored glasses, letting herself see him for what he was. What he always would be. "I've got a full day. If you had warned me, I could have cleared some time."

"Don't patronize me, Sonny. I can see for myself what's going on." He swung the chair back to look at her. "I didn't like the expense report on the wiring."

Once the problem with Miller's wire had been resolved, the price had increased. "You know we only use the finest."

"I'm not telling you to use substandard, Sonny." His voice grew more harsh. "I'm telling you to find it cheaper."

She wondered if he enjoyed doing this to her in front of an audience. The men standing silently next to his chair found other places to look while the confrontation was going on. But they were listening. As was everyone else within range. "That *was* the cheapest I could find."

"Miller and Jones. Didn't look very far, did you?" For the first time he turned his frosty gaze on Angelo. "He turn you on to it?" Miles jerked a thumb at Angelo.

Angelo didn't change his expression. Only Allison saw his jaw harden. "And good day to you, too, Mr. Conrad."

Conrad scowled. He wasn't used to being mocked. "I won't have this upstart dragging down our name, Sonny."

Angelo found he had to bite his tongue to keep from making a retort. He was glad Shad wasn't around. Shad wasn't as even-tempered as he was.

Allison clenched her hands at her sides. "Mr. Marino had nothing to do with it. If you'd bothered to read my report, you'd know that I've been dealing with Miller and Jones for quite some time. The problem arose when Miller's son took over."

"That's when all the problems usually start. When the second generation takes over." Conrad saw the color rise in Allison's face. "How much longer are you planning to take?"

She wet her lips, damning him in her heart. But he was her father, so she kept her peace. "Two weeks."

"Make it a week," Conrad snapped. "Fred Sherrill's corporation wants to build a new hotel. I told him we'd get the bid in. If he likes it, we start breaking ground in a month. You'll be heading the project."

"Don't you think she needs some time off?" Angelo asked.

"I'll decide when she gets time off, Marino, not you. She's my daughter."

"Sounds more like she's your slave," Angelo observed easily.

"Angelo," Allison said sharply. This wouldn't lead to anything positive and she knew it.

"Tough talk," Conrad scoffed. "You wouldn't talk to me that way if I wasn't in a wheelchair."

"No, I wouldn't," Angelo agreed. It was hard to hold himself in check. "I would have probably knocked your block off by now."

"Angelo!" Allison cried again. What had come over this easygoing man?

Rage painted Conrad's face. "I'll see you at dinner," he snapped at Allison. Pressing the controls on his armrest, he turned the chair around one hundred and eighty degrees. The two men hurried silently after him.

Allison stared at Angelo. "How could you say that to him?"

The answer was simple. "Because he treated you like dirt. For two cents I would have wrapped my hands around his throat and—"

She almost believed he meant it. "He's my father."

"I know, I know." Angelo paused for a beat, struggling to get his temper under control. "Couldn't I just squeeze him a little?"

She laughed and closed her eyes. The tension was draining. "You're impossible."

"Yeah, but I'm all yours." He rested his hands on her waist, her father's impromptu visit forgotten. "What are you going to do about it?"

Pretense was gone. She had her haven. Allison rested her head against his chest. "Just be grateful, I guess."

He grinned. "You're learning. Took a while, but you're learning."

Chapter Twelve

Adrian Walters walked into the center of the new extension. Glimmering emerald squares danced on the light green and peach tiles on the ground floor below, gliding down on beams shining from the newly installed dome. He was obviously very pleased, even on the first leg of the tour Allison, Angelo and Shad were conducting. The slight man clasped his hands as he turned to them.

"Well, I must say I'm very, very impressed. It all looks absolutely wonderful. And ahead of schedule, too." He beamed. Allison could almost see visions of dollar signs dancing in his head. "We'll have a private gala opening of this section this coming Friday. Black tie, champagne, a grand piano in the courtyard." He looked solicitously at the three people before him. "You'll come, of course?"

"Well, I . . ." Allison's voice trailed off as she hesitated. She didn't care for formal affairs. She wasn't at ease making small talk.

"Of course," Angelo answered for all of them. He looked at the crew in the background. They were busy with the

cleanup. It had been a long haul for all of them, but well
worth it. They'd come in just as they had said, on time and
under budget. That meant bonuses for his men. But Angelo wanted something more for them, another type of re-
ward for a job well-done. "Are they all invited?" He
gestured behind him.

Walters looked over the rim of his glasses past Angelo.
Angelo knew Walters didn't see the men working there as a
construction crew. He saw them as potential shoppers at the
center. People he couldn't snub. "Of course."

Angelo looked at Allison. "Can't say no to that, can
you?"

No, she couldn't. Over the past few weeks she had discovered that she couldn't say no to anything Angelo asked.
He had brought warmth and color into her life with the first
bouquet of forget-me-nots. And she never would forget him.
She realized now, as never before, that hers was a world of
structure and strength, of buildings she could point to with
pride. But she hadn't built anything with her life. He'd been
right about that.

Angelo had been right about a lot of things, she thought
as she continued the tour with Walters, crisply pointing out
variations of the design here and there. This wing was her
side of the new mall, and she was very proud of it.

Yet somehow it all felt hollow. And the hollowness continued to grow as Friday approached.

By the time she reached the mall on Friday night, Allison
was consumed with an overwhelming emptiness. It was over.
This project was over. There was another job waiting for her
on Monday. And soon she would be boarding a plane for
Albuquerque to stand in one-hundred-plus-degree weather
and oversee the construction of a splashy new hotel with the
Sherrill name on it.

And Angelo would be here, having his Sunday dinners,
with someone else sitting in the chair next to him. Her chair.

Trying to keep the misery out of her eyes, Allison threaded her way to the center of the Emerald Plaza. The *Moonlight Sonata* was wafting hauntingly through the air, thanks to the talents of the gaunt, intense-looking musician playing the piano on the ground floor.

The dreamy music intensified her mood. She had never felt this way before at the end of a project. Always before she was anxious to go on, to start something new. This time there was only sadness. She didn't want to let go.

"I'd say a penny for your thoughts, but by the looks of your expression, I think I might have to take out a federal loan."

She turned at the sound of Angelo's voice, then stopped. She blinked, stunned. "Angelo?"

He was amused by her expression and utterly enchanted by her appearance. She was wearing a simple white sheath with diamonds at her throat and ears. They caught the light and shot out sparks. Not unlike the way she did, he thought. She looked regal. It wasn't true that clothes made the woman. In this case the woman made the clothes.

Playing along, he held his arms out to the side for her to survey the total picture. "Yes, it's me."

She looked him over appreciatively. "You're gorgeous."

He pressed a soft kiss to her temple and was pleased when she leaned into it. As if she had been waiting for him. "I could return the compliment, but then I kind of like you in boots and a work shirt." He grinned wickedly. "With nothing else in between."

He was wearing a tuxedo, and she had had no idea that he could look so breathtakingly handsome. The wide planes of his face, which made him appear so rugged on the site, somehow looked softer in this light. He reminded her of a young lion, moving within his pride, conqueror of all he saw. She wanted to run her fingers through his hair but restrained herself. You just didn't do things like that in public.

And then she remembered that she had kissed him in the parking lot of one of the busiest malls in Orange County. With a smile playing on her lips Allison reached up and trailed her fingers through his hair.

He took her hand and kissed her palm, sending a shiver through her, through them both. Wanting her was ripping him up inside. "You know, I rather like that image. And the nothing in between is better. What do you say we do something about it soon?"

For a moment, seeing him, she had forgotten. It would do no good to believe in fantasies. She had made her choice and was bound to it. The smile on her lips faded. "I have to be in Albuquerque by Monday."

He wouldn't let go of her hand. The gentle pressure made her look up into his eyes. "No, you don't have to be. They can start work without you, or your father can send someone else in your place." He had looked into Conrad and Son and knew there were several other engineers attached to the firm who could take over a project for a while.

"He wants me to be there." A waitress dressed in emerald-green, to match the theme of the new extension, stopped to offer them champagne. Angelo inclined his head at the woman as he took two glasses and handed one to Allison.

"I want you to be here."

She smiled sadly. The light coming from the dome was trapped in her champagne. She looked down into it, tilting the glass. Was that what she had? A bit of light in her life that she had captured for a moment? It would go as quickly as it had come.

"For how long?" Tomorrow, or the week after, whatever there was between them would be over. And she'd have the rest of her life to savor the memory and look back on what she no longer had. She needed to work in order to keep going. It was something she could count on to see her through. It had always helped to keep the hurt at bay.

"I thought we settled that in the very beginning." With an elaborate movement he linked his arm with hers and sipped from his glass.

It was romantic and silly and she loved it. And him. God, she would miss him. "What are you talking about?"

"We were discussing how long I wanted you. Keep your mind on the conversation." He took another sip, watching her face as he did. "A man doesn't ask a woman to be the mother of his children and then toss her away like a tissue."

No, she wouldn't let herself believe that he was serious. She wanted it too much to find out it was a joke. "I thought you were crazy then."

He led her to the railing that encircled the center, allowing them to look down at the first floor. "Maybe, but that doesn't alter what I said."

She twirled the glass in her fingers. "Then you were serious?"

He wanted to take her into his arms, to hold her, to touch her. But he stood where he was, letting this play itself out. "Then. And now."

"You want to marry me." She said it as if she was repeating a foreign phrase she was trying to make sense out of.

"I'm a very traditional kind of guy." He grinned, leaning against the railing as he looked at her. He pictured her in bed next to him. He knew he wanted to wake up that way for the rest of his life. He had known that ever since that first morning in the grass. "First marriage, then the kids. Ma'd skin me alive if it was the other way around." She was wearing her hair up in a French twist. He resisted the temptation to pull out the pins.

She shook her head. "I don't understand."

He smiled, amused. "Where did I lose you?"

"Marriage?" she echoed. No one had ever asked her before. She'd never gotten close enough to anyone for them to ask. She found the idea frightened her. And yet ... and yet there wasn't anything else she wanted more.

Angelo took Allison's glass from her hand and placed it on one of the marble benches that lined the railing. He took her hands in his. "I see we're going to have to go slow here." She opened her mouth to protest, but he kissed her quickly to stop any words. It was a method he could easily get used to. "That's okay. I've got all night."

His eyes held hers. The love she saw there made her want to cry.

"Marriage is when two people promise to be there for each other. Marriage means not running away if one of them happens to have a bad day and needs a handy target. It means laughing at things nobody else understands. It means that during those times when the world crashes in around you it's all right because there's someone to hold you in their arms. It means—" He stopped as he touched the damp streak on her cheek. "You're crying."

She sniffed, shaking her head. "Something in the air."

No, it wasn't. But he played along. "That could be my cologne. I'll change it."

How was she lucky enough to have found someone like him? Someone who had hung on while she had tried desperately to push him away? Afraid of rejection, guilty about turning from her responsibilities, all that had been between them and he had stayed through it all. "You're an idiot." She laughed.

He took her into his arms. Nothing had ever felt so good, or so right. "That's the part you're supposed to put up with."

Allison rested her cheek against his chest, not caring who saw. "Do you really want to marry me?"

He raised her chin with his finger. "You're a slow learner, aren't you?" She started to laugh again, even as the tears kept coming. "That's okay. A high IQ isn't mandatory in this case. Just lots of love." He kissed her again. "Love me."

She placed her hand on his chest. The rhythmic beat of his heart beneath her fingertips drove shafts of sunbeams throughout her. "You know I do."

In his heart he did, but he needed the words. Everyone needed to hear them. "No, you never really said it. That *is* mandatory. I need to hear it, Allison. At least once a day." He nipped her lower lip lightly, wishing he could do a lot more, wishing for someplace a little more private than the center of a mall filled with partying people. "In exchange I promise to love you forever and give you every other Mother's Day off."

"I love you," she whispered. It felt wonderful to say the words.

Halfway around the other side of the railing, Shad stood watching his brother and Allison. Walters handed Shad a glass of champagne. He held his own glass aloft, toasting the area. "You have built a magnificent addition, Mr. McClellan, you and the others."

Shad looked over toward Angelo and Allison, who were completely oblivious to the entire world. He smiled as he watched Angelo kiss her. It didn't take a student of body language to see what was happening. "I think we've also just acquired one, as well." He lifted his glass in a silent toast to the couple.

Angelo had wanted to come with her, but Allison had refused. She wanted to tell her father that she was getting married by herself. She didn't want to have Angelo subjected to anything Miles Conrad might have to say. She knew it wasn't going to be a pleasant scene. She only hoped that he wouldn't say anything too cutting.

Her father hadn't come to the party at the mall. Mingling, now that he was in a wheelchair, no longer interested him. Only his work did.

She found him in his study, going over figures when she got in at eleven. She thought of going to bed and telling him in the morning, then decided that she was through setting her life aside for his, through anticipating scenes and holding her peace. She had done it too long and gotten nothing in return.

As always, when she entered the room, he didn't bother looking up from what he was doing. Always his work was first. But now it didn't matter any longer. There was someone else to give her the love she needed with no conditions attached.

She began with no salutation, no preamble. "You're going to have to find someone else to go to Albuquerque, Father."

He looked up then, clearly annoyed at being interrupted before he finished. "Not that you're indispensable, but at the moment there is no one else." Ending the discussion, he got back to his work.

She looked at the crown of his head. He didn't even have the common courtesy to ask her why she had said what she had. There was only his way and nothing else. *Damn you, old man. I gave you everything and there wasn't even a shred of love in you to give me.* "Then you'll have to go yourself. After the wedding."

He let his pen drop. There was disbelief in his eyes. "What wedding?"

"Mine." She saw by his expression that nothing she said could have surprised him more. *Didn't you think anyone could love me, Father? Just because you didn't?*

He pushed himself away from the desk and moved around it until he was in front of her. "To that clown you met on the site? That would be your style."

He could say anything he wanted to her. But she wouldn't let him talk that way about Angelo. "He's not a clown, Father. He's a wonderful, caring man."

Conrad's laugh was nasty. "Who wouldn't be hurt by marrying into this company."

That would be the way he thought, not about love, but about gain. He couldn't understand what it meant to love anyone. "He has a company of his own." Allison's voice was proud.

Conrad's look was disdainfully condescending. "I didn't see it listed in *Forbes* magazine."

All the years she had been an emotional prisoner suddenly rose up before her. Why couldn't he, just once, wish her well? Couldn't he think of her happiness instead of the business? "There's a lot not listed there, Father, like how to have a heart."

He turned his back on her and began to move to his desk. "You're hysterical."

Allison stood in front of the wheelchair and blocked his path. "No, I'm thinking clearly for the first time in my life." Drawing her courage to her, she risked one more rejection. "I'd like you to give me away at my wedding, or at least be there." She saw the answer in his eyes and moved aside, letting him pass. He wouldn't come to the wedding. "Giving me away should be easy for you, Father. You never wanted any part of me to begin with." Although she had known it in her heart, it hurt to say the words out loud.

"I took you into the business."

"After I forced you," she reminded him. "I only did that because I wanted you to notice me. Wanted it so badly that I would have done anything, been anything, just to be a part of you. To have you care." She dragged her hand through her hair. Pins scattered on the oriental rug. She left them where they fell. She finally accepted the fact that there would never be any communion between them, any feelings on his part. "But you were always too busy to care. Now you can come to my wedding and be my father, or you can stay here and go on being a bitter old man. The choice is yours. I'm finally making mine."

"You'll be sorry."

"No, I've *been* sorry. Sorry all these years that I couldn't please you, couldn't be what you wanted. I've found someone who cares about me and I'm not letting him get away. I almost drove him away because of you. I'm not going to do that anymore."

She saw she'd shaken him. He'd never dealt well with emotions, and Allison regretted that her happiness made him uncomfortable.

"You can marry that idiot or not, but I don't have to be subjected to this rudeness."

Without another word Allison turned on her heel and walked out of the room.

Miles threw the only threat he knew in her path to keep her from leaving. "But if you do marry him, you're through with the company."

She didn't bother turning around as she squared her shoulders. "Your loss, Father," she promised, "will be greater than mine." And she walked out quickly. She didn't want him to see her tears.

Allison didn't want Angelo to see her crying, either, but he did. Worried about her when she didn't phone, Angelo called the house half an hour later. Edna told him that Allison and her father had had an argument. Allison had left the house.

The spa was closed, so Angelo looked for Allison at the mall. The security guard hadn't seen her return after everyone left. At his wit's end, Angelo decided to try her office, even though it was after midnight.

He found her there, sitting in her chair, looking out the window. Having bottled up everything for so long, she couldn't hold back the tears any longer.

Hearing a noise, she turned around, expecting to see the night watchman. When she saw Angelo standing in the doorway, she quickly wiped her tears away with the back of her hand. "What are you doing here?"

He came in. She'd been through a lot, but he knew better than to sweep her into his arms. He had learned that affection was something Allison had to be taught to accept gradually. She didn't have his background. "Looking for you."

"But the building is closed. How did you get in?"

He sat on the corner of her desk. Didn't she realize by now that nothing stood in his way when it meant getting to her? "I had a talk with the guard downstairs." It had taken most of his charm, but he had managed to get in. "I told him that you and I had had a fight and he let me in. He believes in romance."

She shook her head in disbelief. "Too bad Adam and Eve didn't have you to intervene for them in the Garden of Eden. We'd still be wearing fig leaves."

He smiled at her, his eyes sliding over her body. She was still wearing her white sheath. "It's something to consider." Soothingly he ran his hand through her hair. "I talked to Edna. Want to change your mind about the wedding?"

She saw the compassion in his face and shook her head fiercely. "Never that."

He let out a sigh of relief. He'd been worried. Now that that was settled Angelo realized she had been emptying out her drawers. "What's all this?" He nodded at a boxful of books.

"I'm packing." She smiled weakly. "He fired me."

It was beyond Angelo's comprehension. "His own daughter?"

She rose, needing to do something with her hands. She started to pack again. "I'm not his daughter. A man would have feelings for his daughter. I'm just someone with the same last name." She realized she hadn't come to terms with that, even though she thought she had. But she was trying to. "A scapegoat for when he's angry at the world."

Angelo took the book from her hands and drew her into his arms, forgetting to go slow. There was too much hurt in her eyes. "Look, we can take all the time in the world. If you feel that going to Albuquerque for him would make him more receptive, we can postpone the wedding." He never wanted her to regret the step she was taking.

She shook her head. Now that she'd agreed she wanted it to happen as soon as possible. "I've been waiting twenty-nine years to feel this kind of rush." She brushed a kiss against his lips. It made her feel safe. "I want to marry you as soon as possible, Angelo, and put the rest of this all behind me."

Angelo held her against him. Much as he loved her he knew she wouldn't be happy this way. Not with things left up in the air.

An hour later, after leaving Allison safely at Dottie's house, he drove up to the Conrad estate. It was almost two in the morning, but he didn't care. He kept ringing the doorbell until Edna came to answer the front door.

She stood before him, clutching her beige robe to her, her eyes a little foggy from sleep. There was surprise and concern written on her face.

"Edna, I know it's late, but I've got to speak to Mr. Conrad."

"Has something happened? Is she all right?" Edna had confided her worries when Angelo called earlier. She told him that she had never seen Allison like that.

He placed his hand comfortingly on her old, wrinkled one. At least Allison had had someone in the house who cared. "She's fine. I took her to my sister's house. We're getting married next week." He smiled at her. "She'd like you to be at the wedding."

Edna opened the door wide, letting him enter. "Nothing could keep me away." She turned and led the way to Conrad's room. "This way, please."

Miles Conrad wasn't asleep. In the background the strains of Mozart's music filled the room, coming from an elaborate sound system.

"He plays that when he can't sleep," Edna told Angelo as she brought him to the bedroom door. "Has his own devils, I imagine. But none he didn't have a hand in creating." She stepped aside, then patted Angelo on the shoulder. "Good luck," she murmured, shuffling off.

Angelo knocked once, then turned the knob, walking in without waiting to be admitted.

Miles looked up from his bed, startled. The remote control in his hand fell on the bold purple velvet quilt covering the king-size bed. "What the hell do you want?"

"I want to talk to you."

"Edna!" Miles cried loudly. When she peered into the room, he pointed at Angelo. "Call the police. I want him out of my house."

Edna shook her head. "Sorry, Mr. Conrad. I have a cold. I think I'll go back to bed." So saying, she shut the double doors behind her and withdrew.

Angelo could almost physically feel the hatred in Conrad's eyes. It was like a wall he couldn't breach. But he had to try for Allison's sake.

Miles turned up the music, determined to ignore him. Angelo took the remote control from him and shut the sound system off. "I'll be brief."

Trapped, Miles crossed his arms. "Not brief enough."

"You mean like the attention you've given Allison."

Conrad's head jerked up. "What I do with my daughter is none of your business."

"I think it is." Angelo's voice was mild, even though he was seething inside. "I'm going to marry her and see if I can salvage the sweet woman you've tried to destroy all these years."

Conrad's wrath had always made the people around him cringe, but Angelo wasn't disturbed by his angry exclamation. "How dare you!"

He fixed the older man with a hard look. "Now I don't know why, because you've twisted her life inside out, but she wants you at the wedding."

"I don't attend disasters."

Two could play at word games. Dottie had trained him well with her banter. "You've attended your own life, haven't you?"

Rage colored Conrad's face. "I've made a success of my life."

Angelo almost laughed incredulously. "By throwing away the only thing of value you ever created?"

"Philosophy from a construction worker?" Miles scoffed nastily.

If he was trying to belittle Angelo, he had failed miserably. Angelo was his own man and his worth wasn't subject to what Miles Conrad thought or didn't think of him. "It doesn't take much philosophy to have a heart, Mr. Conrad." He tried one last time. "Look, it would mean a great deal to her to have you at the wedding and I want her to have a chance at happiness. Can't you put aside your own self-consuming meanness for one day and come for Allison's sake? She's devoted her whole life to you. Can't you devote an hour to her?"

It was like talking to a wall. Swallowing an oath, Angelo dropped the remote control onto Miles's bed and left the room.

Miles turned up the volume full force.

It didn't help drown out the words that kept echoing in his head.

Chapter Thirteen

It was crowded in the tiny room Saint Anthony's had set aside for the bride. With everyone in it Allison hardly had space to turn around. It was madness. After feeling alone so much of her life, she suddenly had four sets of hands helping her.

"How are you holding up?" Dottie asked, unzipping the long garment bag that contained Allison's ankle-length chiffon wedding dress. Bridgette took the dress out and carefully arranged it for Allison.

"Fine," Allison lied as butterflies conducted full-scale dogfights within her. "I should be asking you that."

"What?" Dottie followed Allison's glance to her stomach. "Oh, you mean that." Although there were absolutely no signs of her pregnancy evident, Dottie spread her hand over her abdomen protectively in a timeless gesture. "I'm past the icky part. Now all I can think of is 'feed-me.'" She grinned, ducking out of the way as J.T. moved toward Allison. "I'm really looking forward to the reception."

J.T. glanced at her watch. "There isn't going to be a reception if the bride isn't ready on time."

"I'm ready," Allison said. She thought of Angelo, of his kindness, of the way he had put her feelings ahead of his the night he had proposed. "Really ready."

"I know Angelo would marry you stark naked, but I think the rest of the congregation might require something a little more substantial than a white slip," J.T. murmured. She opened a compact with several shades of eye shadow in it. "Here, let me put your makeup on."

Allison laughed, reaching for the compact. "I can do my own makeup."

J.T. held it aloft. "No bride can do her own makeup on her wedding day. It's a scientific fact." She eased Allison into the only chair in the room. "Their hands shake." With careful strokes J.T. applied the slightest touch of blue to each lid and then smudged it with her fingertip. Just as she began to put on the mascara, there was a knock on the door. Allison turned her head. "Hold still," J.T. chided.

Bridgette Marino pushed her way past her granddaughter and her daughter-in-law to get to the door. "Who is it?"

"Angelo."

Bridgette opened the door and held it ajar. "You know it is bad luck for the groom to see the bride before the wedding."

Angelo glanced down at the Great Dane at his side. Dottie had groomed Fate and tied a huge bow around his neck. It was ice-blue to match the bridesmaids' dresses.

"Even if the groom has the bride's dog?" he asked his mother.

Bridgette opened the door a crack and eased out. Her heart warmed when she saw her son. She only wished Salvator could have lived to share this with her. Glancing at Fate, she tried to look stern. "A dog in Saint Anthony's." She shook her head. "You are lucky that Father Lawrence is so easygoing."

Angelo knew his mother had moved heaven and earth to arrange a wedding so quickly. "Father Lawrence wouldn't dare go against anything you asked for." Fate barked once and licked Bridgette's hand. "Besides, if it wasn't for the dog, you wouldn't be getting your wish."

She petted the animal's head. "Take him to Shad and make sure he ties that ring tightly. I have waited over thirty years for this day and I do not want to see anything go wrong."

Angelo kissed her cheek. "I love you, Ma."

She smiled, blinking back tears. "I know. Go, go." Bridgette waved her hand at him.

He wrapped the leash once around his hand and went to find Shad as Bridgette closed the door. Well, it had been worth a try. He had wanted to get one peek at Allison before the wedding, just to assure himself that she was there and really going to go through with it. He had known all along that she would, and yet a part of him had trouble believing it was finally happening.

He found Shad, Frankie and Shea milling around the side entrance of the church.

Shad placed an arm around his brother's wide shoulders. "Need anyone to prop you up?"

"Nope." Angelo grinned, handing over the dog's leash to his best man. "I'm fine."

Shea was skeptical. As much as he loved Dottie, there had been last-minute jitters before the wedding. "Hold your hand out," he instructed. When Angelo did, Shea examined it closely. "No tremor." He was surprised.

"I told you." Angelo stuck his hand into his pocket. "I'm not nervous." And he wasn't. He had waited for the nervousness that had come over Shad and then Shea as each had taken his turn at the altar. But it hadn't come. He had never been so deadly calm, so sure of anything in his life. The only thing he worried about was that something would happen to shatter all this.

Angelo looked at Shad, remembering his mother's last-minute instruction. "You have the ring?"

Shad dug it out of his pocket and held the diamond-encrusted band aloft. "J.T. made me check three times before we left the house."

Angelo nodded. "Don't forget to tie it to Fate's collar."

Frankie moved forward. "Uncle Angie?"

Angelo turned and smiled warmly at his nephew. In his pearl-gray usher's suit he looked more like a man than a boy. "Yes?"

"If you're not nervous, how come you keep looking at the door?" He nodded toward the front of the church.

Angelo hadn't thought he was that obvious. He'd been hoping that Miles would change his mind at the last minute and come. Angelo had always been an eternal optimist. "Just waiting for someone to show." He exchanged looks with Shea, who slowly shook his head. He knew, Angelo thought. "Doesn't look like he's going to."

"Someone important?" Frankie asked.

"He is to Allison." Angelo could have throttled the old man, but it wouldn't have done Allison any good. He promised himself to make it up to her. She was never going to regret marrying him.

With J.T. on one side of her and Dottie helping on the other, Allison slipped on her wedding dress. It felt as if she were slipping into a dream. The material was soft and delicate and floated down around her like a cloud. She had no idea how the new women in her family had managed everything so quickly.

It had been a matter of divide and conquer. Dottie handled the clothes. J.T. the hall and invitations. Bridgette the church and the food. It was a family that knew how to work together for a common goal. And she was going to be part of it. She couldn't believe it was really true.

"I wish you had picked something with a zipper instead of a thousand tiny buttons," Dottie murmured, working her way down Allison's back.

"Here, let me." J.T. nudged Dottie gently aside. Gratefully Dottie sat down. "But she's right, you know," J.T. told Allison. "Angelo might just rip these off with his teeth if he loses his patience." She cast a glance over her shoulder at Bridgette, suddenly remembering the woman was there. But Mrs. Marino only smiled.

When the last button was slipped into its loop, Alessandra begged to be allowed to help Allison put on the headpiece. Just as she finished, organ music filtered into the tiny room.

"I think that's our cue." J.T. squeezed Allison's moist hand. "It's going to be fine," she whispered, slipping out of the room.

Dottie hugged Allison. "He's a great guy, Allison. I could always count on him to be there for me. Shad would yell and bite my head off, but Angelo always tried to set it right. He's a rock."

Yes, he was. Her rock. She had come to understand that. No matter what happened he would be there for her. She had never had that before. She was luckier than she had ever dared hope.

Allison nodded. "I know."

Dottie stepped back to allow Alex some room. "You look beautiful," Alex whispered, pressing a kiss on Allison's cheek.

Allison caught a glimpse of herself in the mirror. She was glowing, glowing because she was marrying Angelo. "I feel beautiful."

And then there was only Bridgette left in the room. The older woman fussed a little with the veil, spreading it out around Allison. Then she looked at Allison, love shining in her eyes. "I love all of my children, Allison. When first

Shad and then Dottie were married, I rejoiced. And each time I said to Angelo, 'Why not you, too?' He never answered. But now I know why not.'' She took Allison's hands in hers and held them for a long moment. ''He was waiting for you.'' Bridgette smiled as tears threatened to fall. ''I am glad he waited.'' She kissed Allison. ''Be happy.''

Allison squeezed the woman's hand, so full of love, so full of happiness that she could hardly understand it all. ''I will. I promise I will.''

Bridgette took a handkerchief from her tiny purse. ''I hate women who cry at weddings. There is no reason to cry. Weddings are happy times.'' She sniffed and left as her eyes filled with tears.

The wedding march was starting. Allison took one final look at the mirror, then gathered her dress and left the room. Although both Shad and Shea had offered to walk down the aisle with her, she had politely but firmly refused. She had gone through life alone; she would walk down the aisle alone. Her heart still ached that her father hadn't wanted to attend, but she had come to terms with his absence. She realized now that she should have come to terms with it years ago. She wouldn't have tried so hard.

With the doorway of the inner church in sight, she thought she heard someone whisper her name in the vestibule. Just nerves.

But when she heard the voice calling her again, she knew it wasn't her imagination. She turned slowly, afraid to hope, afraid to believe. He had disappointed her so many times over the years.

But Miles was there, slowly coming toward her, his hand pressing the controls on the armrest. His expression was stern.

Had he come to ruin this for her? Ruin this the way he had ruined so many other small triumphs, always finding fault, finding the flaw. Allison lifted her chin. She wasn't going to let him do that to her anymore.

"Hello, Father, lost your way?"

This was hard for him. Harder than accepting his disabling condition. But he knew what was at stake if he didn't try.

"Yes, yes, I have. It was pointed out to me the other night that I was throwing away the most precious thing I had ever created." The threat of permanently losing Allison had made everything else suddenly seem so empty. "I tried to deny that, but the more I denied it, the more I realized that it was true." He looked at her, hoping she would understand. "A man's legacy is his children. He lives on in their memories of him. This isn't easy for me to say, but I know that yours aren't very favorable."

He cleared his throat. "I know I haven't the right to give you away because you were never really mine. I saw to that." He placed his hand on hers awkwardly. They never really touched over the years, but he needed that human contact now. He couldn't get back the years that had passed. He didn't want to lose the ones ahead. "But I'd like the opportunity to place your hand in the hand of someone I know can appreciate you the way you should be appreciated." His lips curved. It was a slight smile, but it was a start. "Love you the way you deserve to be loved."

She knew how much this had cost him. All the wrong that had been done melted away. She only saw him as he was now. "Oh, Father." She blinked hard, trying to keep her tears back. She blessed J.T. for her waterproof mascara.

"Everything all right out here?" Shad peered out into the narrow vestibule, looking from Allison to the man in the wheelchair. The wedding march had ended and then begun again. "Angelo thinks you're having second thoughts, and Fate is about to eat the ring."

Allison looked down at her father. "Everything's just perfect."

Shad let out a sigh of relief. "Then let's get this show on the road." Waving a hand toward the front of the church, Shad was answered by the beginning strains of the wedding march. "They're playing your song, Sonny."

"Allison," her father corrected. "From now on it's Allison." Miles turned his chair so that he was facing the middle aisle. Allison rested one hand on his shoulder, and they began to move forward. "By the way, I talked Sherrill into postponing the ground-breaking on the hotel for three weeks. The job is still yours if you want it."

Grinning, she matched her gait to the steady pace of the wheelchair. "I want it."

"And perhaps, after the honeymoon, you and your husband would like to consider a different sort of merger. One involving our two companies." He smiled at her. "There's enough business out there for all of us."

Everything. She was getting everything in one wonderful swoop. He had done this, Allison thought as she slowly walked down the aisle. Angelo had somehow arranged this to come about. She knew it. He was a stubborn man, the man she was marrying. She blessed him for it now for so many reasons.

"Who gives this woman away?" the priest asked.

"I do," Miles answered in a voice that was surprisingly tender.

Tears gathered in her eyes again as her father placed her hand in Angelo's.

Angelo and Allison turned together to face the priest at the altar.

"I don't know how to thank you," she whispered to him, her lips scarcely moving.

Angelo winked, wishing he could kiss her now instead of at the end of the ceremony. "I'll think of something," he promised.

A thrill went through her. She had no doubts about that. After all, Angelo was always as good as his word. Allison's heart swelled as she listened to the words that signaled the beginning of the rest of her life. The best part.

*   *   *   *   *

**Three All-American beauties discover
love comes in all shapes and sizes!**

ALL-AMERICAN SWEETHEARTS

by Laurie Paige

CARA'S BELOVED (#917)—*February*

SALLY'S BEAU (#923)—*March*

VICTORIA'S CONQUEST (#933)—*April*

A lost love, a new love and a hidden one, three
All-American Sweethearts get their men in Paradise Falls,
West Virginia. Only in America... and only
from Silhouette Romance!

Silhouette
R O M A N C E™

SRLP1

HE'S MORE THAN A MAN, HE'S ONE OF OUR

Fabulous Fathers

HAUNTED HUSBAND
Elizabeth August

Thatcher Brant, widower and father of two, was so busy keeping the peace in Smytheshire, Massachusetts, he hadn't time to think about romance. But this chief of police was in for quite an awakening when his childhood nemesis, Samantha Hogan, moved into his house. How could Thatcher have ever guessed that fate would bring Samantha—the woman he had never dared care about—close enough to touch?

Find out if the best things in life truly come to those who wait, in Elizabeth August's HAUNTED HUSBAND, available in March.

Fall in love with our FABULOUS FATHERS—and join the Silhouette Romance family!

Silhouette
ROMANCE™

FF393

SPRING FANCY

Three bachelors, footloose
and fancy-free... until now!

Spring into romance with three
fabulous fancies by three of
Silhouette's hottest authors:

ANNETTE BROADRICK
LASS SMALL
KASEY MICHAELS

When spring fancy strikes, no man is immune!

Look for this exciting new short-story collection
in March at your favorite retail outlet.

Only from

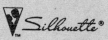

SF93

where passion lives.

**Silhouette Books
is proud to present
our best authors,
their best books...
and the best in
your reading pleasure!**

Throughout 1993, look for exciting books
by these top names in contemporary
romance:

CATHERINE COULTER—
Aftershocks in February

FERN MICHAELS—
Whisper My Name in March

DIANA PALMER—
Heather's Song in March

ELIZABETH LOWELL—
Love Song for a Raven in April

SANDRA BROWN
(previously published under
the pseudonym Erin St. Claire)—
Led Astray in April

LINDA HOWARD—
All That Glitters in May

When it comes to passion,
we wrote the book.

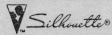

BOBT1R

Take 4 bestselling love stories FREE

Plus get a FREE surprise gift!

Special Limited-time Offer

Mail to Silhouette Reader Service™

3010 Walden Avenue
P.O. Box 1867
Buffalo, N.Y. 14269-1867

YES! Please send me 4 free Silhouette Romance™ novels and my free surprise gift. Then send me 6 brand-new novels every month, which I will receive months before they appear in bookstores. Bill me at the low price of $1.99* each plus 25¢ delivery and applicable sales tax, if any.* I understand that accepting the books and gift places me under no obligation ever to buy any books. I can always return a shipment and cancel at any time. Even if I never buy another book from Silhouette, the 4 free books and the surprise gift are mine to keep forever.

215 BPA AJCL

Name	(PLEASE PRINT)	

Address	Apt No.	

City	State	Zip

This offer is limited to one order per household and not valid to present Silhouette Romance™ subscribers. *Terms and prices are subject to change without notice. Sales tax applicable in N.Y.

USROM-93   ©1990 Harlequin Enterprises Limited

For all those readers who've been looking for something a little bit different, a little bit spooky, let Silhouette Books take you on a journey to the dark side of love with

SILHOUETTE
Shadows™

If you like your romance mixed with a hint of danger, a taste of something eerie and wild, you'll love Shadows. This new line will send a shiver down your spine and make your heart beat faster. It's full of romance and more—and some of your favorite authors will be featured right from the start. Look for our four launch titles wherever books are sold, because you won't want to miss a single one.

THE LAST CAVALIER—Heather Graham Pozzessere
WHO IS DEBORAH?—Elise Title
STRANGER IN THE MIST—Lee Karr
SWAMP SECRETS—Carla Cassidy

After that, look for two books every month, and prepare to tremble with fear—and passion.

SILHOUETTE SHADOWS, coming your way in March.

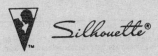

Silhouette®

SHAD1